Desperate Measures

Patricia H. Rushford

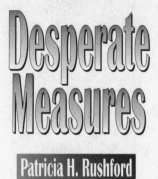

Blessings

Patricia H Rushford

Books by Patricia Rushford

Young Adult Fiction

JENNIE MCGRADY MYSTERIES

1. Too Many Secrets
2. Silent Witness
3. Pursued
4. Deceived
5. Without a Trace
6. Dying to Win
7. Betrayed
8. In Too Deep
9. Over the Edge
10. From the Ashes
11. Desperate Measures
12. Abandoned
13. Forgotten
14. Stranded
15. Grave Matters

Desperate Measures

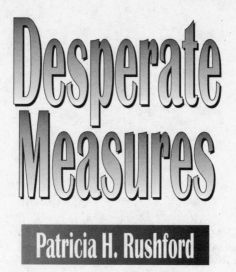

Patricia H. Rushford

BETHANY HOUSE PUBLISHERS
MINNEAPOLIS, MINNESOTA 55438

Published by Bethany House Publishers
11400 Hampshire Avenue South
Bloomington, Minnesota 55438
www.bethanyhouse.com

Bethany House Publishers is a Division of
Baker Book House Company, Grand Rapids, Michigan.

Printed in the United States of America

ISBN 0–7642–2080–2

Acknowledgments

Thanks to the Fur Commission, fur farmers, and animal preservation groups for contributing to the authenticity of *Desperate Measures*—most specifically to Arnold Kroll, Judy Frandsen, Jan Bono, and the Clark County Medical Examiner's office.

PATRICIA RUSHFORD is an award-winning writer, speaker, and teacher who has published numerous articles and over twenty-seven books, including *What Kids Need Most in a Mom*, *The Jack and Jill Syndrome: Healing for Broken Children*, and *Have You Hugged Your Teenager Today?* She is a registered nurse and has a master's degree in counseling from Western Evangelical Seminary. She and her husband, Ron, live in Washington State and have two grown children, eight grandchildren, and lots of nephews and nieces.

Pat has been reading mysteries for as long as she can remember and is delighted to be writing mysteries of her own. She is a member of Mystery Writers of America, Sisters in Crime, and several other writing organizations. She is also the co-director of Writer's Weekend at the Beach.

1

The gun barrel dug deep into Jennie McGrady's ribs. She pushed it away and tried to concentrate on the paper she was writing on acid rain.

"Bang! I got you." Nick stepped back and fired again.

"Ow!" She jumped when the cold water soaked through her T-shirt and ran down her side. "Mom!" Jennie yelled. "Tell Nick to leave me alone. He's being a pest."

She'd tried everything she could think of to get her five-year-old brother out of her hair, but he kept coming back. Ordinarily she didn't mind having him around, but today was not one of those days. This day, this no-good, horrible, not-worth-getting-up-for day, she wanted to be left alone.

"Oh, for heaven's sake, Jennie," Susan McGrady countered, "if there's a problem with Nick, take care of it yourself. I'm trying to rest."

Guilt crept in with all the other bad feelings rolling around inside. Mom, being newly pregnant, needed her rest. She'd been suffering off and on with serious bouts of morning sickness.

"Why are you telling Mommy on me?" Nick wrapped his scrawny arms around her neck and climbed on her back, nearly choking her. "Don't you love me no more?"

"Nick, please." Jennie could hear the whine in her voice and didn't like it one bit. She was acting more like six than sixteen. Jennie pulled him around to her lap and gave him a hug. "I love you. It's just that I'm in a rotten mood."

"Why?"

"Because," she said simply, then listed the reasons in her

7

mind. *Because Ryan Johnson is a jerk. Because our school was burned to the ground in an arson fire and we have to go to school in an old warehouse in Oregon City. Because I have to do twice as much work around the house as usual. Summer's nearly over and it's raining.*

Jennie could have named half a dozen more becauses, but what good would it do? All the complaining in the world wouldn't change the fact that Ryan was dating Camilla, and Jennie had slipped back into the role of being *just* a friend. She'd seen the beginnings of a romance between Ryan and Camilla during her last visit to her grandparents' home in Bay Village at the coast where Ryan lived. Ryan had assured her then that there was nothing between them. *Yeah, right.* Jennie thought back to her conversation with Ryan the night before.

"We'll always be friends, Jennie," Ryan assured her. "Right now I don't even know how I feel about Camilla," he said, "but we've been out a couple of times and—"

"You don't have to explain," Jennie mumbled. "I understand. I feel the same way about . . . Scott." Jennie wasn't sure why Scott Chambers came to mind at that particular moment, but he had and with good results.

"The guy you met in Florida?" Ryan sounded jealous.

"Yeah." Jennie picked up Scott's picture from her dresser.

"I guess that means he finally got ahold of you," Ryan said.

"What do you mean?" She set the picture back.

"While your gram and J.B. have been gone, I've been picking up the mail and getting phone messages. He sent a letter to her address with your name on it and left about three messages on her answering machine."

"Scott did? Why didn't you call me?"

"I didn't realize it was that important to you or I would have." Jennie bristled. "It is. As important as Camilla is to you."

"I see. Then I guess we don't have much more to say to each other."

"I guess not." Jennie hung up. Too angry to cry, she tried to put the entire conversation out of her head.

So far she hadn't had much luck. She pushed thoughts of Ryan away again now as Nick looked at her with his pleading dark blue eyes. Those eyes and thick, dark hair, so like her own, were a genetic trait from the McGrady side of the family. Jennie, Nick, Jennie's dad, Jason, his twin sister, Kate, and Gram all had similar features. Of course, Gram's hair was now mostly gray.

Setting Nick on the floor, she tried one more time. "Nick, I need to study. And I think I hear Bernie calling you."

Nick listened intently. "I don't hear him." Bernie was Nick's St. Bernard puppy, though as big as the dog had gotten over the summer, the puppy part didn't do him justice.

"That's because you're not listening with your heart," Jennie explained. "Trust me, Bernie wants you to play with him."

"He always knocks me down. You come play too."

"I can't. I have homework, then I have to get ready to go with Lisa." Jennie glanced at the clock. Lisa Calhoun, her cousin and best friend, would be calling any minute and wanting to leave. Unfortunately, Jennie wasn't anywhere near ready.

"Where ya goin'?" Nick wriggled off her lap, looking as if he were about to cry.

"Lisa and I are spending the weekend with Megan."

"At the mink farm?" He jumped up and down. "I want to go too. Can I go? I want to see the baby minks."

"Not this time."

"I'm going to ask Mommy. She'll make you take me."

"Good idea." Jennie grinned at his departing figure, got up, and closed her bedroom door. Mom would say no, of course. With any luck at all, she'd distract him with a story. The weekend away was Jennie's reward for putting in all the extra hours working around the house the last few weeks.

Back at her computer, she tried concentrating on her report, but part of her brain stayed focused on the weekend. Tom and Mary Bergstrom had been family friends for years, and their daughter, Megan, invited them out to the farm several weekends a year.

Looking forward to the outing and wondering why Scott had called kept Jennie from feeling too depressed about Ryan. She sighed and forced herself to concentrate on her project—writing about the effects of pollution on rivers and streams and how fish and wildlife are affected by human carelessness. Deformed fish were showing up in some of the local rivers. Not a good sign.

As Jennie worked, Scott Chambers slipped into her mind again. After managing to write two pages, she gave up and moved to her window seat. Images of Florida and Scott became too strong to ignore. Jennie remembered their first meeting and how she'd thought him arrogant and overly committed to his animal rights activist group, the Dolphin Protection Agency. He'd been on a save-the-dolphins kick and practically accused her of being a dolphin killer because she and Gram were going to see the dolphins and sea lions perform at Dolphin Playland. Even in those first stormy moments, though, she'd felt a certain attraction to him. After he learned that Gram was researching and writing articles on the subject, he warmed considerably, and over the course of two weeks, Jennie and Scott had become good friends.

Jennie's heart still fluttered at the thought of his intense sea-green gaze boring into hers during their first meeting. He had a killer smile and loved to tease her. She admired his determination to save the dolphins but worried about his overzealous attitude. Jennie loved dolphins, too, and planned to do what she could. On the other hand, it was Scott who piqued her interest in environmental issues, which had led her to concentrate on term papers like "Dolphins in Our Midst," "Cigarette Butts and Their Impact on Marine Life," and "Acid Rain."

Why had Scott been trying to call her? Had he come out west to go to school? He'd mentioned coming to the area to study marine biology. She mentally kicked herself for not getting Scott's number from Ryan. "No way am I going to call him back now."

Jennie sighed. Gram was due home in another week. "You'll find out soon enough," she told herself. For now, however, she needed to concentrate on her homework.

An hour later, Jennie saved her file, backed out of her word processing program, and turned off her computer. She'd just placed her duffel bag on the bed when the phone rang. Thinking it was Lisa, she answered, "I'm almost ready."

"Ready for what?"

"Oops. Sorry, I thought you were . . . Scott?" Jennie tipped her head back, glad he couldn't see the silly grin on her face.

"Hey, you recognized my voice. That's a good sign."

"I heard you were tying to get ahold of me."

"Yeah, I lost your number, and all I could find was your grandmother's business card. Ryan called a few minutes ago to let me know she was out of town and gave me your number."

"How nice of him."

"Yeah, it saved me from having to call all the McGradys in the Portland phone book. As I recall, Ryan is your boyfriend."

"Was."

"Hmm. I wondered. He didn't seem too happy about sharing your number. Asked me a bunch of questions first."

"Like what?"

Scott laughed. "If you can believe it, I think he wanted to make sure my intentions were honorable. He must still like you."

Jennie shrugged off the hurt she felt over Ryan's dating Camilla. "Probably habit. We've been friends a long time." Wanting to change the subject, she asked, "So why have you been trying to get ahold of me?"

"I moved out here a couple weeks ago. Too late for first semester, so until I can get into Oregon State, I signed on to do a research project for an animal ethics group. People for the Protection of Animals—ever heard of them?"

"No." Jennie bit her lip, not sure she really wanted to know but knowing she should ask anyway. "What are you researching?"

"The treatment of minks among fur ranchers in Oregon."

Jennie groaned. "You're kidding. I can't believe this. Some friends of ours own a mink farm near Lebanon. Lisa and I are visiting there this weekend."

"Yeah? Who?"

"Tom and Mary Bergstrom."

"Really? Wow. Must be fate, Jennie. I just got a job with the Bergstroms. Figured the best way to do research was some hands-on experience."

Jennie should have been delighted. She would get to be with Scott again for an entire weekend, but the thrill of seeing him drowned in the trepidation she felt. Scott Chambers working on a mink farm, where over ten thousand mink were caged and bred for their coats, oil, and body parts, could only lead to one thing. Trouble.

2

"Do you really think Scott will do something bad?" Lisa asked after Jennie confided her concerns about Scott's working on the mink farm.

"Not bad." The rain had given way to partial sunshine on their drive south on I–5. They'd drive through Lebanon, then turn toward Thompson, which was located just east of the Bergstrom farm. Jennie flipped on the air conditioning in her red Mustang. "He's not malicious, just misguided, I think. When I first met Scott he'd been arrested four times for going too far in protecting dolphins and other marine life. I know how much he hates people using dolphins like circus animals, so think how he must feel about killing fur-bearing animals like mink and fox so people can have fur coats and oil to protect their shoes."

"Probably not real crazy about the idea, huh?"

"How do you feel about breeding animals for their fur?" Jennie asked.

Lisa turned in her seat and tucked her leg up under her. "Megan's parents have had the mink farm since I can remember. I love the feel of real fur. Still, it's always bothered me that those poor animals have to die."

"Me too. But like Mom says, how much different is it from raising animals like ostrich, bunnies, lambs, and cows to slaughter for food and hides?"

"Not to mention the hunters who go after deer and elk just for fun."

"And seals," Jennie added.

"At least the Bergstroms take good care of their animals." Lisa sighed. "Didn't you say Scott was just researching?"

"That's what he told me." Jennie moved into the right lane and drummed her fingers on the steering wheel. "I hope that's all he's doing."

"I saw in the paper where one of those animal-rights groups picketed a store back east. They put on full-length mink coats all splattered with blood and locked themselves in cages right in front of the store." Lisa wrinkled her nose.

"That's disgusting," Jennie said. "Wonder where they got the blood?"

"Good question. Do you suppose they killed an animal to get it?"

"Hmm. I doubt it. That would go against their principles."

"Maybe they take it from each other."

Jennie grimaced. "I think I read someplace where a group of them broke into a blood bank and stole human blood."

Lisa gasped. "That's awful. Seems like they care more about animals than about people."

"I'm not so sure they care that much about the animals either. Some of the things they do hurt humans *and* animals. If I were a mink farmer I'd be worried—especially after an activist group released all those mink this summer. That farm wasn't too far from Tom and Mary's."

"You mean the one where all those mink died?" Lisa asked. "The paper said the death rate was in the thousands."

"Yeah, and most of them were babies that hadn't been weaned yet."

"Makes me furious. How could they say they want to help the animals and then do something that ends up killing them? It just doesn't seem right."

"It's senseless and stupid." Jennie left the interstate, taking the highway east to Lebanon. "I feel bad for the animals that are killed, but like Gram always says, 'Two wrongs don't make a right.' Besides, I'm not convinced using animals for food and clothing is wrong. People have been wearing animal skins since God first created humans. In Genesis it says God gave the man and woman clothes made from the skins of animals. He meant for us to use animals for food, but I'm sure He wouldn't sanction abuse."

"I guess it's one of those issues that doesn't have any easy answers."

"Well, I refuse to worry about it," Jennie decided. "All I want to do this weekend is relax and have a good time. This is our last long weekend before fall."

"Ditto. Did you bring your swimsuit?"

Jennie laughed. "That's like asking if I brought my skin." Jennie loved swimming and had joined the swim team at Trinity High. Their coach, DeeDee Dayton, made them practice at least once a day, but this weekend DeeDee was going sailing in the San Juan Islands.

You kids have a free weekend, the coach had told them at practice the day before.

Friday was a state-wide teachers' conference, and with Monday being Labor Day, they had a four-day weekend. Jennie planned to enjoy every minute of it. She tried to think of her reunion with Scott as part of the fun, but her intuition kicked in again, giving her the uneasy feeling she always had just before something disastrous was about to happen.

Ten minutes later, they turned onto a long, tree-lined driveway that wound to the top of a hill. The farm was only about twenty acres—it didn't take a lot of land to raise fur-bearing animals. But because mink had a faint odor reminiscent of skunk, Tom and Mary had built their new home on the hill, about a football field's length away from the barns. Jennie's gaze settled on the fenced-in area where the mink were raised. She'd been inside with Megan and Mr. Bergstrom several times.

The mink were housed in ten long, metal barns about 430 feet long, each containing fourteen hundred wire mesh cages. In front of the barns was a large, rectangular two-story metal shop where the Bergstroms kept their farm machinery and mixed the mink's feed—a high-protein concoction of chicken, beef livers, and grain. It looked like canned cat food.

Halfway between the mink and the new house was an older two-story farmhouse—where the Bergstroms used to live. They now used it to house the hired hands who worked for them. Scott would probably be staying there.

Jennie stopped the car, got out, and looked around. Her gaze panned the outbuildings, but she saw no sign of Scott.

"Jennie! Lisa!" Megan threw open the front door and rushed toward them, arms open wide, her blond curls bouncing up and down. "I can't believe you're finally here."

Drooley, their dog, lumbered down the steps, woofing in that deep, casual way basset hounds did. They'd named him Drooley because that's exactly what he did—drooled and slobbered all over. Megan called it wet kisses. Though she wasn't crazy about all the slobber, Jennie liked Drooley and gave him a warm greeting. She rubbed his ears and looked into his huge, sad eyes. "Hi, boy. Did you miss us?"

He woofed in response and slobbered all over her hand.

"Go say hi to Lisa." Jennie wiped her hand on her pant leg.

Lisa got out of the car and stepped into Megan's open arms. "We'd have been here sooner, but Jennie wanted to do her homework first. Isn't that sick?"

Megan laughed. "Very. I probably won't get to mine until midnight Monday night." Megan's round face, soft blue eyes, and wide, dimpled smile reminded Jennie of a Shirley Temple doll. She was Lisa's height—five two, which made her six inches shorter than Jennie.

"You two are just jealous." Jennie hugged Megan, bent down to pet Drooley again, then opened the trunk.

"You're right about that," Megan said, "but no more talking about homework for the rest of the time you're here. That's an order."

"Sounds good to me." Lisa hauled her bag out of the backseat.

"We are going to have so much fun. I made reservations for us at the English Rose in Thompson for high tea tomorrow afternoon. Then tomorrow night we'll have a swimming party and barbecue, and later on we can roast marshmallows and s'mores and sit around the campfire telling scary stories. I've invited three guys." Megan grabbed a couple of bags from the trunk and started toward the house.

"Sounds cool except for the guys," Lisa said, giving Jennie a knowing look. "I've sworn off men for good."

Megan set the bags in the entry of their large two-story Victorian and gave Lisa a look of disbelief. "You?" She giggled. "What happened? Did you get dumped?"

"Not exactly. Let's just say I'd just as soon not have a boyfriend for a while."

"I can understand that, but it's not like you have to get serious or anything. Anyway, it's just Scott Chambers, a really cute guy who works for us, my boyfriend, Algie Summers, and his best friend, Kyle Baxter."

"Algie?" Jennie and Lisa asked in unison.

"I know, isn't it an awful name? His parents named him Algernon, after a great-uncle or something. You get used to it after a while. He's really sweet. Scott told us he met you in Florida while he was working there, Jennie. I thought you'd be happy about my inviting him. I *know* he wants to see you."

"I'm looking forward to seeing him again too." Jennie took a deep breath, wondering how much Scott had told them about his past. Probably not much, she decided, or he would never have gotten the job. "You've gone to a lot of trouble to set things up."

"It's not every day I get to have you guys out here." Megan turned a concerned gaze to Lisa. "You'll like Kyle. It won't be like a date or anything. But if you think you'd feel too uncomfortable, I could cancel and we could do something by ourselves—like watch a couple videos or . . ."

Lisa shrugged. "No problem. I'll survive. Besides, I'd like to meet Algie, and I definitely want to meet Scott."

"Speaking of Scott," Jennie said, "where is he?"

"Next door interviewing Mr. Sutherland."

"Interviewing?"

"He's doing an independent study with Oregon State—part of the fur-farming program. The Sutherlands raise mink too. Though why Scott wants to interview Bob Sutherland is beyond me. You remember them, don't you?"

Jennie nodded. While she liked Christine Sutherland, she remembered her husband, Bob, as being unpleasant and rude.

"I hope Scott's okay." Lisa glanced toward the Sutherland farm. "From what you've told me about him, Jennie, he and Mr.

Sutherland would be about as compatible as oil and water."

"You're right about that," Jennie said. Mr. Sutherland was not only a fur farmer, but also a hunter. Something Scott despised. "Megan, did Scott tell you why he was doing the research?" Jennie had a feeling his research involved more than some project for school. He'd said he was working with People for the Protection of Animals. Suppose he was spying for the activist group that took credit for freeing the mink this summer? What if he was helping them plan another attack? *Come on, Scott. Please, don't cause any trouble.*

Megan shook her head and brushed a stray curl out of her eyes. "I'm sure he'll be fine. Mr. Sutherland likes showing off his mink. He won an award last year for having the best facility in Oregon. Oh, and I have to tell you the latest. Remember his daughter, Aleshia?"

Jennie nodded. Aleshia looked like a high-fashion model—tall and slender with thick, dark hair and turquoise eyes, probably the result of colored contacts. She had a hard edge, though, like her father.

"Well," Megan went on, "Aleshia hates the fur-farming business—always has, I think. Now she's designing a whole line of fake furs and is making megabucks."

"Really? I thought she was still in college." Jennie leaned against the railing.

"She quit. She had to get a job because Mr. Sutherland kicked her out."

"Why? Because she doesn't agree with him?" Jennie could identify with being at odds with a parent. But she couldn't imagine Mom kicking her out because they didn't share the same views.

"I guess. But you have to understand, Jennie, Aleshia doesn't just disagree. She joined this fanatical activist group that Dad says is nothing but a bunch of criminals using animals as an excuse to commit terrorist acts. Anyway, that was the group who released the mink this summer near Mt. Angel. Aleshia says she didn't have anything to do with the release. She had an alibi but told everyone she agreed with whoever did it."

"Whew. I guess I can see why her parents would be upset." Lisa pulled her long red-gold hair into a ponytail and slipped a scrunchie around it. "Where is she now?"

Megan lifted her shoulders in an exaggerated shrug. "Living in Portland somewhere, I think."

Jennie pulled her thoughts from Aleshia back to Scott. "And you think Scott is safe over there?"

"Sure. Hey, you don't think he's a spy for ARM, do you?" Megan asked.

"Arm?" Lisa and Jennie asked at the same time.

"Animal Rights Movement. He told us he was doing a project with the experimental fur-farming program at Oregon State. But if you think he's lying or might be scouting our places for ARM, I should let Dad know right away."

"He didn't say anything about ARM to me." Jennie wished she could talk to Scott and find out what he was really up to. Until she could, it was best not to jump to conclusions. "Um—why don't we put our stuff in your room and do something fun. Like swim."

"Sounds good to me." Megan picked up the bags and walked through the tiled entry and to the stairs. "Mom and Dad are at a meeting tonight, so it's just the three of us. We can swim for a while, then drive into town for hamburgers or order in pizza."

"Pizza," Lisa said.

"That sounds good to me too." They followed Megan up the stairs to her bedroom. Jennie set her bag down just inside the door. The room was big and had a walk-in closet. Colorful quilts covered the beds, along with an assortment of stuffed animals and pillows in every color imaginable.

"I love your room." Lisa twirled around and plopped down on the bunk beds she and Jennie would share.

"Me too, most of the time. When I'm in a bad mood, though, it's not so good. It's too cheerful."

Jennie chuckled. "Maybe that's the idea."

The girls changed into bathing suits and headed down the hill toward the five-acre lake that bordered both the Bergstrom and the Sutherland properties. The lake was clear and cold, fed by an underground spring. The Bergstroms had built a dock and diving raft, which allowed swimmers to avoid the rocks and slimy plant life around the periphery. At the other end of the lake was a boat ramp and drive that led to the Sutherlands' property. A small silver motorboat sat atop the ramp on a trailer.

The girls swam until dusk, then headed back to the house to order pizza. Jennie lingered in the bedroom after Megan and Lisa had showered and dressed and gone downstairs to wait. She sank onto the lower bunk. It was dark now and still she'd seen no sign of Scott. He wasn't shy, and he knew she was coming, so why hadn't he come to the house to at least say hello?

"Jennie?" Megan called from the bottom of the stairs. "Are you okay?"

"I'm fine. Be down in a minute." Jennie rose and went to stand in front of the window, wishing she could shake the growing uneasiness rising inside her. Maybe she should go out to the barns to see if Scott was there.

No, she decided. *He's probably busy feeding the animals or something. Of course, he might still be talking to the Sutherlands. Come on, McGrady. Stop worrying about him. Scott's a big boy. He can take care of himself.*

Headlights flashed as the pizza-delivery van pulled into the driveway. Jennie set aside her concerns about Scott and gave in to her growling stomach.

3

The girls ate a sausage, mushroom, and pepperoni pizza and popcorn while they watched *While You Were Sleeping*. After the movie, they were about to head upstairs to bed when they heard a motorcycle come up the driveway.

"That must be Scott." Megan jumped up and peeked through the blinds. "Yep. It's him—he's headed this way."

Scott marched up the porch steps and rang the doorbell. Jennie's heart shifted into overdrive. Megan went to answer it while Jennie and Lisa picked up their trash, popcorn bowls, plates, and glasses and carried them to the kitchen.

"Jennie," Megan called from the entry in a singsong voice. "Someone's here to see you."

Jennie's heart took a tumble, trying to keep up with the butterflies in her stomach.

"Scott, hi." Her voice sounded deceptively normal as she joined him in the entry. She resisted the urge to hug him and instead introduced him to Lisa.

"Hi." Lisa's gaze drifted over him.

"Hey. Good to finally meet you." Scott grinned and winked at Jennie. "You were right. Her eyes are the same color as mine."

Jennie felt a twinge of jealousy. Lisa was so feminine and cute. Most guys liked her instantly. She glanced up at Scott, but he was no longer looking at Lisa. In fact, he hardly seemed to notice her at all.

"So, Jennie. Solved any crimes lately?"

"A few."

"I'd like to hear about them."

They talked for a few minutes about their mutual friends at Dolphin Island, then to escape her giggling cousin and friend, she suggested they go outside.

Scott grinned down at her and stuffed his hands in his jeans pockets. "You . . . um . . . you look great."

"You too." She let her gaze swing from the floor to his broad shoulders and green eyes. In fact, he looked better than great.

When he might have kissed her, she ducked away and headed for the porch swing. It was a lot like the one sitting on her own front porch, and Jennie suddenly needed something familiar. She dropped into it and set it swinging. "So, where have you been all day?"

"At the fur farm next door and out to Corvallis. Oregon State has an extension program there." He sat down next to her, resting his arm across the back of the swing. "Did you miss me?"

"Sort of. If you must know, I was afraid you might be getting into trouble."

He laughed and settled his arm around her shoulders, pulling her toward him in a friendly hug. "Relax, Jennie, I'm not going to do anything illegal."

She leaned back and arched an eyebrow. "Are you sure? I happen to remember a couple of incidents in Florida."

"Yeah, don't remind me. You'll be happy to know I'm a reformed man. I'm not into the extremist animal rights groups anymore." He released her and clasped his hands in front of him. "'Course, I haven't changed my mind about protecting animals either. I just don't think bombing labs and research centers is the answer."

"What made you change your mind?"

Scott stared at his hands, then lifted his gaze to hers. "There's a group called ARM. I was with them for a while. They were dedicated to saving animals from research centers. Awful things are done to animals in the name of research like injecting them with a live AIDS virus or cancer cells or sewing their eyes shut so these so-called scientists could study the effects of blindness."

Jennie winced. "That's terrible. People really do that?"

"Yep. So I figure, why not release them? Give them a chance

21

at freedom. At the time I thought it was a good idea, but sometimes ARM goes too far. They torched a research center in Florida and ended up killing two of the firefighters. That did it for me. One of the guys killed in the fire was a friend of mine."

"You weren't . . ."

Scott shook his head and reached for Jennie's hand. "No, fortunately I wasn't there. Scary thing was, I could have been. I had no idea they were going to torch the place. Later, Sonja—the group's leader—said that their deaths were unfortunate but that we needed to look at the fact that two dozen monkeys were on their way to freedom."

"This Sonja person, wasn't she arrested?"

"No. The authorities can't find her. Sonja isn't her real name. She's in hiding, and no one, not even most members of the organization, knows where she is. In fact, she may actually be a man. People hide, move around, and use phony names. Like a lot of terrorist groups, they surface to launch their attacks, then go underground again."

"Hmm. Did you know Mr. Sutherland's daughter, Aleshia, is a member of ARM? From what I hear she doesn't hide it."

"I heard. Sutherland went on about it for about an hour."

"Do you know her?"

Scott shook his head. "I don't think so."

"Well, I'm glad you're not part of ARM anymore. But you're still with an animal rights group."

"Not animal rights, animal ethics. The organization I belong to now lobbies for humane treatment of animals. Which is why I'm working at the mink ranch. I want to see firsthand how the animals are cared for and what happens to them. I don't especially like the idea of using animals for fur, but I'm trying to be impartial—at least for now."

"I'm so relieved." Jennie dropped her gaze to their clasped hands.

"Why?"

She glanced up in surprise. "I don't know. I just am. I don't want to see you end up in jail."

His smile was back. "You care."

"Of course. You're a friend."

"That's good." He leaned forward and kissed her. This time she didn't move away.

"Been waiting all day to do that," Scott said. "It's great to see you again."

"I'm glad you're here." Jennie rested her head against his shoulder.

"I came because of you."

"And school," Jennie reminded him.

He grinned. "Well, that too. I was kind of hoping with Ryan out of the way, we could maybe start going out."

"Hmm, maybe." Jennie bit her lower lip. "I'm not in any hurry to get serious."

"I'm not either. But it would be nice to have a girlfriend to hang out with on weekends while I'm going to school out here."

A car turned into the driveway and stopped in front of the garage. "Looks like Tom and Mary are back." Jennie felt a rush of relief. Scott was starting to make her feel uncomfortable.

After greeting the Bergstoms, Scott excused himself. "I need to make a final check on the mink, then I'll turn in."

"Hang on a minute," Tom said. "I'll walk down with you." His bear-like form enveloped Jennie in a hug. "We'll catch up at breakfast, Jennie. I'm anxious to know how your folks are doing. Your dad still liking his job as a homicide detective?"

Jennie shrugged. "I think so. It keeps him pretty busy."

"How about you? I heard you're expecting a new baby at your house."

"Yeah." Her mom's pregnancy still embarrassed her, but once she'd gotten over the initial shock, she'd been as excited as Nick.

"It's good to have you girls here again. We always enjoy your visits." He turned back to Scott, settling a thick arm across the younger man's shoulders. "So how did your interview with Sutherland go today?"

"Pretty good. I got a lot of photographs. . . ." Their voices trailed off as they walked away.

"When is Susan due, Jennie?" Mary asked.

"Oh, um—April." Jennie dragged her attention back to Mary. "She's got morning sickness right now. Makes me wonder if I'll ever want kids."

"Parts of pregnancy are miserable, but once that baby comes, you forget how bad it was."

Jennie followed Mary into the house. Mary was nearly as tall as Jennie and twice as wide, but not really overweight. She wore her dishwater blond hair in a bun at the top of her head, and several loose tendrils framed her cute, round, dimpled face. It was easy to see who Megan favored.

"I'm sorry we deserted you girls tonight," Mary said, "but we had a prior commitment and couldn't get out of it. Hope everything went all right."

"Perfect," Jennie assured her. "By the way, Mom said to say hi. She'll probably call this weekend."

"Do you think she and Jason would come out for a barbecue Monday afternoon? I'll invite Kevin and Kate as well—it would be wonderful to see them again."

"They'd like to see you too—you should call them."

"Hi, Mom. How was the meeting?" Megan bounced into the front room with Lisa trailing behind, both in pajamas.

"Somber, I'm afraid. A rep from the fur commission told us about another raid on a retail furrier in San Francisco. They firebombed the place. Lost an inventory of around five million."

"Those terrorists sure move around a lot." Crossing her arms, Megan flopped down on the sofa. Lisa dropped down next to her.

Mary slipped her shoes off and lowered herself into a gliding rocker, resting her feet on the matching ottoman. "That's what's so frightening. We never know when or where they'll strike next. The FBI has photographs from protests all across the country. Some of the same faces keep cropping up. They think these guys are paid terrorists who go from one place to another. They have weapons and martial arts training. We were told not to try to confront them."

Megan sighed. "What will we do if they hit us?"

Mary tipped her head back. "I don't want to even entertain that possibility."

"It's hard not to think about it." Megan twisted a ringlet around her finger.

"It would be scary to me." Lisa tucked her legs under her. "Do you ever think of selling and getting into something else?"

"Yes. But that would be giving up, and neither Tom nor I are willing to do that. I hate giving in to these people. We have a right to raise mink just as every individual has a right to wear the fur or use the products we produce without being judged or threatened. There is nothing wrong with what we do."

Jennie sank onto the couch beside Lisa. Though she didn't say it, she found herself grappling with the issue of rights. How far should people's rights go? Did animals have rights too? She certainly didn't agree with the guerrilla tactics ARM used, but she did care about animals.

Thankfully, the conversation turned from mink and animal rights groups to family matters. Jennie and Lisa told Mary and Megan about each family member and how they were doing. The girls headed to bed around eleven. Jennie fell asleep an hour later, brooding about her feelings for Ryan and Scott and thinking about mink and other animals that were raised for the specific purpose of being killed.

4

The only thing worse than waking up to a buzzing alarm clock was waking up to the explosive sound of gunshots.

"What was that?" Jennie sprang from the top bunk and raced to the window. Lisa groaned and turned over.

Megan rubbed her eyes. "What's going on?"

"I heard a gun—at least I think that's what it was."

Lights popped on in the older farmhouse, and searchlights brightened around the compound where the animals were caged. A lone figure ran across the front yard and disappeared in the shadows. Jennie couldn't make out his features. Scott came to mind, but she couldn't tell for sure.

The phone rang. She could hear Tom's gruff voice answering it in the bedroom next to Megan's.

"Be right there," Tom said. A door banged. Heavy footsteps pounded down the stairs.

Moments later, a siren bleated a staccato alarm. Megan scrambled out of bed, jerked off her pajamas, and pulled on a pair of jeans and a sweat shirt. "The mink. Something's happened."

"Megan." Mary knocked on the bedroom door before opening it. "Come quick. Someone released the Sutherlands' mink. We've got to help round them up."

"Coming." She turned to Jennie. "You guys don't need to come if you don't want."

"Wouldn't miss it, would we?" Jennie nudged Lisa, then dressed quickly in jeans, denim shirt, and purple sweat shirt. Within minutes they were heading out the kitchen door.

Megan handed them each a pair of thick leather gloves. "Put these on to protect your hands. The animals will be frightened, and they're apt to bite." She pointed to a corner where several pair of boots were lined against the wall. "Grab a pair of boots. Hopefully you'll find some to fit."

By the time they reached the Sutherlands', half a dozen people along with the sheriff, Tess Parker, had arrived. Jennie immediately liked the woman. Tess Parker was thirty something, medium build, and the no-nonsense kind of person Jennie admired. She talked for a moment with Mr. Sutherland, then pitched in to help.

"Just get them into their cages," Sutherland barked. "We'll sort them out later." Jennie and Lisa followed Megan's lead, scooping up the frightened animals in large nets and placing them in cages. Many of the mink hadn't bothered to escape, choosing instead to curl up inside the small nesting boxes where they would often sleep. With those less adventurous mink it was easy as slipping the box back into the opening at the top of the cage.

The rain started again, turning the yard into a slippery, muddy mess. About twenty people were now running with nets, looking for the elusive mink.

Jennie made a swipe with her net to capture one as it crossed her path. It slipped away. She tried again, catching it, but the action threw her off balance, and she landed on her backside. Rolling onto her hands and knees, Jennie got back up. She rubbed her grimy hands on her pants and took out after another mink. This one sat cowering in a corner of the farmhouse, where the front steps met the foundation.

"Come here, you." Though she'd been told to use the net, she didn't have the heart. Besides, this one was different, and on closer look she realized it was a fox. The animal shivered. It's heart raced as it snuggled against Jennie. "You're tame," she said, holding it close and trying to warm it. "You poor thing."

"I'll take her, Jennie." Christine Sutherland reached for the fox, grasping it by the nape of the neck, then cradling it in her arms.

"She seems tame," Jennie said, stroking the silvery fur.

"She is. This is Sasha, Aleshia's pet. Aleshia raised her. She has the run of the place. All the excitement—it's terrified her. I'll

27

take her inside for a while until things calm down." She frowned. "It's nice of you to pitch in."

Jennie shrugged and patted Sasha's head. "It's okay. I'm glad I could help." She watched Christine duck into the garage, then went back to work.

Several minutes later, Jennie spotted Scott separating a pair of mink engaged in a ferocious fight. Joining him she said, "I wondered if you'd be out here."

"Why?" he grumbled. "You think I'm more likely to let them go?"

"Well, you don't like seeing them in captivity."

"Do you?" He lifted both animals into the net, then stuck each in a separate cage.

"Not really, but—"

"Look, Jennie"—he closed the cage and settled his angry gaze on her—"at one time I might have looked the other way, but these animals have been bred in captivity. They don't have much chance out on their own. Whoever did this wasn't thinking about how it might affect the animals. All they want to do is destroy the fur industry. Maybe that's not such a bad idea, but this isn't the way to do it."

Feeling misunderstood, confused, and annoyed, Jennie went back to work. Several times she vacillated between recapturing the mink and letting them go. Not out of a sense of justice, but she just didn't like the animals. As beautiful as their fur was, they were frightened, which made them mean and smelly. And there were too many of them. Even with all the help, the task seemed impossible.

Three hours later, eight thousand of the Sutherlands' twelve thousand mink and a hundred of the silver fox had been successfully rounded up. Some had escaped, others had died from being stepped on or torn apart by other mink. Still others were hidden in shrubs and high grass and would hopefully be caught in the morning. The press would be alerted to warn residents not to try to pick up or play with the animals and to call the authorities if they saw any. The greatest danger was to children—and to the mink themselves.

"Sure appreciate all your help. Looks like that's all we can do for now," Sutherland told them, then summoned them all to the house. "You're welcome to come up to the house for something hot to drink. The sheriff wants to ask a few questions."

"I'm beat," Lisa murmured. "I want to go back to bed."

"Me too." Megan yawned. "But we'd better stick around."

Jennie, exhausted and badly in need of a shower, wanted to return to the Bergstroms' place, too, but didn't say so. She was more interested in learning the details about the release and hearing what the others had to say. She looked around for Scott but didn't see him.

As they approached the house, Mrs. Sutherland came out to the porch with a large tray of cups. "Coffee or cocoa, anyone?" She set the tray on a redwood table and told everyone to help themselves.

Jennie, being closest, thanked her and picked up a hot chocolate, then moved out of the way. Lisa and Megan did the same.

Sutherland lifted a steaming cup to his lips. "Appreciate all your help, folks. Tess," his weary gaze settled on the sheriff, "we all know who's responsible for this fiasco. What we don't know is how they were able to bypass the new security system. Almost looks like an inside job. We may have a spy in our midst." His gaze moved from face to face and settled on Jennie and Lisa. "Who are you?"

Jennie glanced at Lisa and swallowed. Even though she had nothing to do with the crime, she felt guilty. Tom slipped between Jennie and Lisa, bringing his arms up to rest on their shoulders. "They didn't have anything to do with this, Bob. For one thing, they were asleep, and for another, they're our guests. They're practically family."

Sutherland rubbed his forehead and frowned. "They could still be spies."

"Lighten up, Bob," Tess said. "Let's not be getting into an argument here. I'll ask the questions and conduct the investigation."

"All right. But whoever did it knew the security system," Sutherland said. "They disarmed the alarms and grounded out the electric fence, then cut openings in the fence just like they did at Jake's place. Well-planned release—must have been a team of a dozen. From what I could tell, people wearing combat boots made the tracks. They pepper-sprayed the dogs and knocked out one of my men." He glanced at one of the men who'd been rounding up the released mink. "Stan's got a tough head or we'd probably all still be sleeping. He fired the rifle to alert us. I activated the house alarm and called Tom and Sheriff Parker."

Sheriff Parker turned to Stan. "Can you tell us what happened? Did you see anyone?"

"'Fraid not." The older man shook his head, a lock of gray hair falling to his forehead. "Thought I heard a noise round the back of the compound and went to investigate. Turned the corner and somebody ambushed me." He rubbed the back of his head. "Don't know how long I was out, but when I woke up, mink were running around all over the place."

None of the others were able to add much, and most of them went home. The sheriff wrote down a few names and phone numbers and asked several to come into her office the next day to give their statements. Everyone but Stan had been asleep—or so they said. She stopped in front of Jennie. "Looks like you really got into this thing."

Jennie glanced down at her sweat shirt and grimaced. It was covered with mud. She doubted the stains would ever come out.

"Come on, Tess." Sutherland moved to the side and rested a hip on the porch railing. "This is a waste of time. Let's get out there and find these guys. The longer we wait the harder it will be to track them."

"Just take it easy, Bob." Sheriff Parker's weary gaze moved back to Sutherland. "I'm inclined to think ARM sent people in here from outside the area. Might have had a few locals, but chances of finding them are pretty slim."

"Right, but they had to have planted a mole—someone who knew where everything was." He rubbed his hand across the wide bald spot on the top of his head. "Tom, what about that new kid you hired? He was over here this afternoon taking pictures and asking questions. Said he was hooked up with the fur farming extension program at Oregon State. I figured you checked him out."

"I did. Called over to the university before I hired him. Also checked his references. He was working at the Dolphin Research Center in Florida before he came here. They had nothing but good things to say about him." Tom set an empty cup on the tray. "I doubt he'd do something like this. Interviewing you in the afternoon and letting your mink out the same night wouldn't be a smart move."

"Anybody out here seen Chambers?" Sutherland glanced around.

"Yeah," Stan said. "He was helping to round up the mink for a while. Left about twenty minutes ago. Said he had some work to finish up over at your place."

"Come on, fellows," the sheriff interrupted again. "We'll get to this guy in a minute. I'm nearly finished here, then we can let these kids go home." Tess turned back to Jennie. "Did you see or hear anything prior to the release?"

"No, I was asleep. The gunshots woke me up, and I looked out the window. I . . . I saw someone—" Jennie hesitated, remembering. Should she tell them it might have been Scott? *No*, a voice inside her warned. *You didn't see him clearly. You only thought it was him. It could have been anyone.*

"Did you recognize the person? Man, woman?"

"No—um—I think it was a man, but I'm not sure. I only saw him for a second and then he was gone. It was dark. . . ."

Tom flashed her an angry look. "You saw someone in our yard and didn't tell us? Jennie, didn't it occur to you they might have hit us as well?" He set his cup down and jumped off the porch.

"I'm sorry. I forgot." Jennie felt miserable. Had the person she'd seen been one of the terrorists? Had they released the mink on their farm while everyone was over here? "I didn't have any idea they might . . ."

The two men looked at each other. "Let's go."

Sutherland scrambled down the stairs and took off running. Jennie's stomach felt like it had turned to stone. Had the person she'd seen crossing the yard been Scott? Could he have been lying to her? Would he? Jennie took a deep breath. She didn't want to know the answer.

"Hold on a minute," the sheriff yelled. "Don't go running off half-cocked." When they didn't stop, she mumbled something unrepeatable and sprinted after them.

"I guess we'd better go too." Mary sighed. "Thanks for the coffee, Christine."

"Sure. Let me know if you need help over there." Christine Sutherland was a wiry woman, with wide hazel eyes and a nice smile. Her thick graying hair curved under at the ends in a modified pageboy. She brushed her bangs aside.

"Appreciate the offer," Mary said, "but to be honest, if someone released our mink, I'd be tempted to just let them go. At least until morning. I'm too tired to deal with them right now."

Christine smiled. "Better not let Tom hear you say that. I know what you mean, though. Sometimes you wonder if it's worth it. It's gotten to be a dangerous occupation."

"Hmm." Mary gave Christine a sympathetic look. "How's Aleshia?"

"Doing very well." Christine's eyes shone with a mixture of hurt and pride. "Her designs are very popular—in fact, she's just put out a catalog. Hang on, I'll get you a copy." Christine ducked inside, then brought out a catalog moments later and handed it to Mary.

"My goodness. This looks impressive."

Jennie caught glimpses of fabulous-looking fake furs as Mary flipped through it.

"Just don't let Tom see it. And don't tell Bob I gave it to you. He'd be furious if he knew I'd even mentioned it."

Jennie frowned. "Mrs. Sutherland, can I ask you a question?"

Christine moved her gaze to Jennie. "Sure."

"Are you on Aleshia's side?"

Christine licked her lips. "It's been heartbreaking to see Aleshia involved with a group like ARM—especially for Bob. I suspect her political agenda has more to do with rebelling against her father than anything. They have always been at odds. But I love my daughter, Jennie. And I'm proud of her." She ducked her head and brushed tears from her eyes. "I think secretly Bob is, too, but he would never admit it."

"Maybe someday they'll make up." Mary gave her a quick hug. "We'll pray for their relationship to heal."

"Thank you." She sucked in a deep breath and picked up the tray, now laden with empty cups. "They're a lot alike, you know."

Tucking the catalog under her arm, Mary promised to look through it more thoroughly later. After saying good-bye, she herded Megan, Jennie, and Lisa back to the house.

There was no sign of Tom or Mr. Sutherland, Sheriff Parker, Stan, or the other workers. No sign of Scott either.

"The pickup is gone," Mary said. "I wonder what's going on?"

A young man emerged from the mink compound and jogged toward them. Jennie recognized him as Jim Owens, one of the men who'd helped recapture the mink and one of Tom and Mary's employees.

"Is everything okay down there?" Mary asked when he approached.

"Yep. No problem as far as I can see. Everything's secure."

"Where's Tom?"

"He and Bob left with the sheriff a few minutes ago. They were going to take Tess back to her car and see if they could find the Chambers kid."

5

"Scott left?" Jennie's heart leaped to her throat.

"His bike's gone. Looks pretty suspicious. They're thinking he may have been in on the release. Wouldn't be surprised."

"Why would you say that?" Jennie asked.

Jim shrugged. "Just seems like the type."

"Scott isn't the type to hurt animals."

"No, but he's an animal lover. And a former member of ARM." Jim brandished the information like a sword.

"He told you that?" Jennie frowned.

"Aleshia told me."

"Aleshia? She knows him?" Jennie's threadbare faith in Scott wore even thinner. Had he lied about that too?

"Apparently." Jim voiced her own thoughts.

Mary slipped an arm around Jennie's shoulders. "We shouldn't speculate on anyone's guilt or innocence at this point. I'm sure the criminals involved with the raid escaped immediately. Besides, I trust Tom's judgment. He wouldn't have hired Scott if he thought there'd be a problem."

"Don't forget," Lisa added, "Scott helped round up the mink."

"I'm sure he had a very good reason for leaving," Mary added. "Now, I suggest we go inside and get cleaned up. Maybe we can still get some sleep."

"Good idea," Lisa said. "I'm so tired I could sleep for a week."

"Me too," Megan echoed.

"I'll see you folks later," Jim said. "Think I'll try to catch a few winks myself."

Jim tossed Jennie an odd look before heading off to the house. Did he know about the connection between her and Scott? It was like he knew something she didn't. Or maybe he was just checking her out.

She was still mulling over the conversation when she stepped out of the shower. As much as she wanted to reserve judgment and give Scott the benefit of the doubt, she found herself growing more and more suspicious and angry. Scott had said he didn't *think* he knew Aleshia. But what if he did? What if he'd worked with her before? Or worse, what if he still was?

Had Scott lied to her about no longer being involved with ARM? If Aleshia knew Scott, had she talked him into coming to Oregon so she could plot revenge against her parents?

Knowing she'd never be able to sleep, Jennie dressed in a clean pair of Levi's, a T-shirt, and a baggy blue sweater instead of her pajamas. While she dressed, another part of her conversation with Jim drifted back. According to Jim, Aleshia had told him about Scott's involvement with ARM. The question now burning in Jennie's mind was when and why had Jim talked to Aleshia?

After towel drying her hair and fixing it into one long braid, Jennie followed the scent of sizzling bacon downstairs and into the kitchen.

"You couldn't sleep either, huh?" Mary turned pieces of bacon over in the pan and covered it with a lid. "Want some orange juice, coffee, tea?"

"Juice sounds good but I can get it." Opening the fridge, she pulled out a pitcher of juice and poured some into the glass Mary handed her. "I'm too worried about Scott to sleep." Jennie snagged a barstool with her foot and sat down.

"Hmm. I guess I'd be concerned too."

"Mary, how well do you know Jim Owens?"

"Very well. He grew up around here. Been working on fur farms since he was a kid. His parents used to own a ranch about ten miles from here. They retired, sold the place, and moved to Florida. Jim had to move out. He was working for the Sutherlands until Aleshia joined ARM. When Bob kicked Aleshia out, he fired Jim."

"Why would he fire him—was Jim part of the organization too?"

"Oh no. Jim completely disagrees with their tactics, but Aleshia and Jim are engaged to be married. Bob feels like both of them have betrayed him. He wanted Jim to break off the engagement with Aleshia. When he refused, Bob told him to leave."

"Sounds complicated. How did he end up working for you?"

"He came over right after he was fired. We needed the help." She shrugged. "We've known him for years."

"Doesn't it seem strange that he'd stay engaged to someone who thinks so differently?"

"Not really. You've heard the saying 'Opposites attract,' haven't you?"

"Yeah—my mom and dad are pretty different." Jennie rolled her eyes thinking about them.

"Well, Aleshia and Jim may be opposite, but they love each other. They are willing to accept each other's differences—I think that's an admirable trait in both of them."

Mary set the bacon on paper towels and began cracking eggs into a bowl. "Would you like an omelet?"

"Sure."

"Cheese, mushrooms, onions, tomato, peppers okay?"

"All except the peppers, thanks," Jennie answered.

The crunch of gravel drew Jennie's attention outside. "Mr. Bergstrom is home." She held back the urge to run outside and tackle him with questions.

"Tom!" Mary rushed into the entry to greet him. "What's going on? Did you find Scott?"

"Yeah." He shook his head. "I still can't believe it. Looks like Scott conned us good. He didn't bother to tell us he'd been a member of ARM up until a month ago. He also has an arrest record in Florida for charges of eco-terrorism." Tom came into the kitchen and dropped his jacket over the back of a chair. "Did you know about that, Jennie?"

"I . . . I knew he'd been arrested before, but—"

"Save it. I wish he had come clean with me. And you, Jennie. I'm disappointed you didn't say anything."

"Tom, you're not being fair. Jennie had no way of knowing what was going on."

"I'm sure you're right, but convincing Bob of that will be another matter. He's sure Scott headed the raid and believes Jennie is somehow involved because she knows him." Tom washed his hands in the sink.

"Do you know where Scott is now?" Jennie asked.

"Yeah. In jail."

"Are you sure Scott did it?" Her legs turned spongy. She collapsed in a chair at the table.

"He claims not. I'd like to believe him, but look at his record. What else are we supposed to think?" Tom dried his hands on a towel hooked to the refrigerator door, poured a cup of coffee, and sank heavily into the chair opposite Jennie.

"Where did you find him?"

"About a mile east of the freeway."

Jennie groaned. "So he was running away?"

"Sure looked that way to us. He claimed he was heading into Salem to meet a friend."

"Did he say who?"

"Nope. He wouldn't tell us where he was going or who he planned to talk to."

"I'm really sorry, Mr. Bergstrom. I wish I'd said something."

"Don't blame yourself, sweetie." Mary slid an omelet onto a plate, added a couple pieces of bacon and toast, then set it down in front of Jennie. "You had no way of knowing."

Jennie stared at her food, not certain she could stomach any of it. What she found even harder to stomach was Scott's betrayal. If that's what it was. "That's not quite true. I had a bad feeling something like this would happen. I trusted Scott." She sighed. "He told me he'd quit ARM because a friend of his was killed during one of their raids."

"Really?" Tom leaned forward, his elbows on the table. "I'd like to hear more about that."

Jennie relayed the story Scott had told her about the arson fire at the Florida lab. "Scott said he didn't have anything to do with it and I believe him. He's not malicious."

"Tell me how you happened to hook up with him."

Jennie picked at the omelet and told him about Florida and Scott's efforts to keep dolphins from being exploited. As she replayed his story, she found herself taking his side again. "I talked to him during the rescue operation over at the Sutherlands'. He seemed really angry about the release. Said whoever did it was hurting more animals than they were helping."

Tom leaned back as Mary brought his omelet. "Thanks, hon." Picking up his fork, he waved it at Jennie. "He's right about that. So what's your take on all of this, Jennie? Do you think he was in on the release?"

Jennie closed her eyes and visualized Scott's sincere green gaze. She remembered how much he loved the dolphins and how shaken he'd been when one of them died. "All I know is that he really cares about animals and the environment. He got fired from a harbor cruise job because he got into an argument with a tourist who helped himself to some live coral." Jennie hoped she wasn't saying too much but felt honor bound to defend him.

"If he was innocent, why did he run?"

"I don't know—maybe he was scared. He knew you'd find out about his arrest record. He probably figured he didn't have a chance."

"Running just makes him look guilty." Tom shoveled in a few bites of omelet.

Jennie couldn't argue with that. She concentrated on getting the food on her plate to her mouth. What had started out as a fun-filled weekend with friends was fast becoming another complicated mystery. Not something she was a stranger to. Jennie had helped solve a number of criminal investigations over the summer. Now she found herself plunked down in the middle of another.

Mary settled into a chair. "When is Scott's arraignment?"

"Tess figured it would be this morning. Thought I'd go in. If you really believe in this guy, Jennie, maybe I should talk to him again." Tom sipped at his coffee. "Would you like to come along?"

"Yes." Feeling more hopeful, Jennie finished her breakfast. She was pretty good at picking up on whether or not someone was lying to her. She hadn't gotten that feeling at all with Scott when they'd been together the evening before. But maybe she was just trying to convince herself that a friend wouldn't lie to her.

6

When he'd finished his breakfast, Tom announced he was going down to help Jim feed and water the mink. Jennie donned boots and a jacket and went along. They started at the far end of the barns and worked forward. While Jim washed out the drink containers and refilled them, Jennie and Tom drove separate mini tractors down the aisles of each barn, placing a dollop of food on each pen. The mink pressed their noses to the one-inch wire mesh, curious about Jennie and eagerly awaiting their meal. Their fur, a deep gray with a lavender tint, was thick and rich and would make beautiful coats. The Bergstroms raised blue iris mink, and each pelt would bring about fifty dollars. Mary had a jacket made out of blue iris fur. Jennie had seen it the last time she'd visited and at Mary's insistence had tried it on. She had never worn anything so luxurious.

Now as she moved from cage to cage, Jennie wondered if she'd ever be able to wear a mink coat. She wondered how God would feel about these animals being used to make outerwear. Then she wondered if maybe God had created them for this purpose. And mink oil was just about the best product available for keeping leather soft, pliable, and water resistant. She used it all the time on her leather hiking boots.

"I'm going up to the house to shower, Jennie," Tom announced before taking his tractor into the shop. "Go ahead and finish your row and put the equipment away. Jim can give you a hand if you need it. We'll leave in about thirty minutes."

When Tom turned to talk to Jim, Jennie continued down the

39

row. Over the noise she heard Tom say something to Jim about putting down a hundred pelts that day. Their voices faded, and Jennie was thankful she didn't have to listen. One hundred of the mink she'd helped to feed would die today.

"That would be the hardest thing about farming," she mumbled to a sleek mink that eyed her as she passed by. Seeing the animals you've raised, whether they were cattle, chicken, pigs, or mink, taken to slaughter.

When she finished her row, Jennie drove the tractor into the shed and parked it in a section where several other vehicles and pieces of equipment were stored.

"Hey," Jim said as he followed her inside, "thanks for all the help. With Chambers taking off like he did, we're shorthanded. Don't suppose you want to stick around and help me skin mink?"

Jennie grimaced. "No, thanks."

"Bothers you, huh? Bothers Aleshia too. I think that's the main reason she hates this business."

"I guess I'm not cut out for this kind of work."

"It's no different than skinning a rabbit," Owens went on. "And the animal doesn't feel anything. We put them to sleep first."

"I wouldn't want to skin a rabbit either." Jennie walked with Jim into the main part of the shed. "I heard you and Aleshia are engaged."

"Yep. We're getting married in June."

Jennie glanced at her watch. She still had twenty minutes before she and Tom would leave for town. "Would you mind if I asked you some questions?"

"Not at all. We can talk while I work." They walked back into a cubicle containing a cart stacked with small wire cages. Against the wall stood a rectangular wooden box that looked like a large coffin on stilts. The cone-shaped metal sheet coming out of it was about a foot wide at the top. Next to the box, mounted to the wall, was a tall blue cylinder that had gauges on top, like the kind hospitals used for oxygen.

Jim attached the hose from the box to the tank. "It's carbon monoxide," he answered the question before Jennie could ask it.

"Carbon monoxide, but that's . . . deadly."

"Exactly." His smile faded. "Oh. I take it Tom never showed you our little gas chamber."

"Um, no, he didn't."

"We place the mink inside, then fill the box with carbon monoxide gas. Only takes about thirty seconds or so. It's painless and quick. They don't suffer."

"Um—I think I'd better go." Jennie had heard far more than she wanted. Her stomach rolled and pitched, almost causing her to lose her breakfast all over the shop floor.

"Thought you wanted to ask me some questions," Jim called after her.

"I'll catch you later when you're not so busy." Jennie managed to get outside and haul in several deep breaths. Her stomach quieted down, deciding to keep its contents intact.

Though she didn't have time for another shower, Jennie washed up and changed clothes for her trip into town. She smelled like mink and felt anything but elegant.

———

Megan and Lisa were still asleep at nine-thirty when Tom announced he was ready to go.

"Looks like it's going to be another nice day," Tom said as they stepped onto the porch. Jennie agreed. The sky was a brilliant blue with smatterings of puffy white clouds. The only dark clouds were those hanging in her heart over Scott's possible guilt. Jennie climbed into Tom's truck, a white Ford Ranger, and snapped the seat belt in place. Glancing through the rear window, into the back of the pickup bed, she noticed a couple of nets and some small cages. "What are those for?"

"Thought I'd better take them along in case we see any stray mink along the way. You can help me keep a lookout. Don't want to hit any. Last release, about thirty-five that we know of ended up as road kill."

"How awful."

He shrugged. "The activists don't consider that when they release the mink. They don't consider a lot of things."

"Will the ones that are loose survive? I mean, what will they do for food?"

"They'll be able to maintain for a short time scavenging on dog or cat food that people leave out, but it isn't what they need. Mink are carniverous, and most of them will just end up dying."

Jennie thought about the gas chamber but didn't say anything. Ending up as fur in a garment had to be better than the kind of life or death release would bring.

"Hang on, Jen—" Tom slammed on the brakes. Jennie would have pitched through the windshield had she not been wearing her seat belt. "Grab a net. There are a couple of critters in the ditch." They picked up four altogether, then piled into the truck again. For three mink lying alongside the road it was too late. Tom picked them up anyway, saying they needed to keep track of as many as possible. They were soon back on the road and headed into town. Jennie's thoughts drifted back to Scott. Apparently Tom's had too.

"If your friend did play a part in the release," Tom said, "he wasn't acting alone. This was a well-executed terrorist act. The sheriff figures there must have been over a dozen people at the very least. Bob's right. They probably had someone scope it out ahead of time."

"And they all got away. It seems like if Scott was one of them he'd have gone with them instead of sticking around to help capture the mink." Of course, he could have helped in order to avoid suspicion, but she didn't mention that.

"I know he's a friend, Jennie, but you must admit it seems pretty strange having him show up here right out of the blue only days before the release."

"Not really. Scott wants to be a marine biologist. He plans to study at OSU. He told me last spring he'd be coming out here." Jennie frowned remembering the woman from Scott's activist group, the Dolphin Protection Agency, in Florida. Melissa had seemed nice enough, but Jennie later learned that she'd asked Scott to infiltrate the Dolphin Research Center and bring back evidence of animal abuse so they could close them down. Jennie felt the organization had been using him to further their program. Could the same thing be happening now?

"I just had a thought." Jennie turned down the visor to block out the morning sun and told him briefly about the incident in

Florida. "It's possible he came to gather information like he said. Maybe that animal ethics group Scott is with didn't tell him what they were planning. He could have been duped into supplying information to the PPA, not knowing they would use it to conduct a release."

"If he really is with them, your scenario won't work. They don't operate that way at all. They advocate humane care of animals, and they aren't out to abolish the fur trade like ARM is."

"Well, there must be some explanation."

"I'm sure you're right. Maybe Tess has been able to find out what it is."

———

The sheriff's office in Thompson, Oregon, population thirteen hundred, was nearly as small as the town itself. The office held a scarred wooden desk, two beige four-drawer filing cabinets, a computer work station, and two chairs. Behind the desk was a metal door with a sign that read, *Jail. Authorized Personnel Only.*

Tess glanced up when they walked in and set aside a folder she'd been looking through. "Jennie. I'm glad you came. Saves me making a phone call."

"Is anything wrong?"

"I have a few questions for you." Looking up at Tom, she asked, "What can I do for you this morning?"

"Just came in to see if you've come to any conclusions about my hired hand."

"No conclusions. I was hoping Jennie might be able to help me out. I keep thinking about the person Jennie saw last night. Any ideas yet on who it was?"

Jennie pinched her lips together. She'd been thinking about the person as well. The height and shape was right for Scott, but she couldn't bring herself to make a positive identification. At least not until she'd talked to him. She shook her head. "I can't say for sure."

Jennie stepped closer to the desk. Papers nearly covered the surface. To one side was a framed photo of Tess and a little boy with the same shade of sandy hair and brown eyes.

"That's Jonathan, my seven-year-old," she answered Jennie's unanswered question.

"He's cute."

"He's a handful, but I love him." She folded her hands and rested her elbows on the desk. "Have a seat."

Jennie lowered herself into a wide wooden chair that looked as though it might have once been part of an oak dining room set. Tess sat on an old wooden swivel chair that rumbled over a hardwood floor when she moved.

"How well do you know Scott Chambers, Jennie?" Tess leaned forward, arms resting on the desk.

"That's a hard question to answer. We spent some time together while my grandmother and I were vacationing in Florida last May."

"How do you feel about ARM? They're the group taking credit for this."

"Taking credit? You mean they admitted it to you?"

"Terrorist groups often leave a calling card. In this case it was in the form of an e-mail message to me. I'm apparently supposed to back off. They claim everyone involved is long gone."

"That's good news for Scott, isn't it? That means he's not part of the group."

Tess tapped her pen against her open palm. "So he claims. His arrest record tells a different story."

"Oh." Jennie bit the inside of her cheek. "I don't think any of the charges were ever proven."

"Are you a member of ARM, Jennie?"

"No." The question startled her. "I didn't even know what it was until yesterday."

"Have you ever been affiliated with an animal rights group?"

Jennie shook her head. "I'm not much for organizations like that. Too busy with school and church."

"How do you feel about fur farming?"

Jennie glanced at Tom. "I don't know. I wouldn't do it myself. I guess it's okay for the ones who do. Why are you asking me all these questions?"

Tess tipped back in her chair, causing it to creak. "Mr. Sutherland thinks you may have been working with Scott as an informant. Perhaps Scott contacted you from Florida and asked if you'd send names and addresses of the fur farmers in the area."

"Mr. Sutherland is wrong. I would never do that. Besides, until yesterday I hadn't heard from Scott since I left Dolphin Island last May."

"But he is your boyfriend."

Jennie frowned. "He's a friend."

"You don't really believe Jennie had anything to do with this, do you?" Tom pressed both hands on the desk and leaned toward Tess. "It seems to me you ought to be questioning Aleshia. If anyone is in a position to inform, she is. Knowing her, she was in the thick of it."

"I'm well aware of that, Tom, but I need to follow up on the leads I have. Besides, Aleshia has an alibi, and Sutherland doesn't think she'd perpetrate a raid against her own flesh and blood."

"Well, you can forget about Jennie here. She comes from a long line of police officers and federal agents. I've known the family for years. Jennie's more apt to solve crimes than commit them."

A thin smile crossed Tess's features. "I'm well aware of Jennie's history. Which is another concern. The last thing I need around here is an amateur detective. The only involvement I want from you, Jennie, is for you to give me as much history about Scott Chambers as possible."

"I've told you all I know about him," Jennie said. "Is he going to be able to get out of jail?"

Tess raised her eyebrows. "He's already gone. I didn't have enough evidence to hold him."

Jennie's shoulders sagged in relief. "When did he leave?"

"This morning. I'm surprised you haven't seen him. Said he was headed back to your place, Tom." She chewed her lip. "Almost wish I'd held him a little longer, though. Sutherland was here about an hour ago, and when he found out I'd turned him loose, he was none too happy. Just hope he doesn't do something we'll all regret."

Jennie stared at Tess. The worried look on her face gave Jennie plenty of cause for alarm. Tom Bergstrom didn't look pleased either. "Come on, Jennie. Knowing Sutherland, he just might be thinking of taking the law into his own hands."

7

"Do you think Scott might have gone back to your place?" Jennie asked.

Tom turned the key, and the truck roared to life. "I wouldn't bet on it. If he did, it was probably to collect his stuff. If he's smart, he'll clear out and not come back. Even if Scott is innocent, it's going to take positive proof to convince Sutherland of it. That man won't rest until we have whoever instigated the release behind bars."

"Mr. Sutherland wouldn't do anything to Scott—" Jennie swallowed hard. "I mean, he wouldn't hurt him, would he?"

Tom stopped at the town's only stop light, then glanced at her. "I don't know, Jennie. Bob is pretty hotheaded. Tends to fly off the handle more often than not." The light changed and Tom eased forward. "Take that business with his daughter. He let his temper get the best of him—disowned her, fired Jim. I know he feels bad about it, but he's a proud man and isn't likely to backtrack or apologize."

"Great. That's just great." Jennie tipped her head back against the hard vinyl seat, giving her mind partly over to praying for Scott's safety and partly to figuring out how to keep him out of jail. Or worse, from getting himself killed. Under the best of circumstances, Scott and Mr. Sutherland would butt heads.

The sun had heated up the cab, and Jennie cranked down the window, letting the brisk morning wind whip around her. Several minutes later Tom turned into the Sutherlands' driveway. A racy teal Lexus with gold trim sat in front of the house.

"Looks like they have company." Jennie unfastened her seat belt when they rolled to a stop.

"Aleshia." Tom's worried look was back.

Jennie took a deep breath. "I thought Mr. Sutherland kicked her out."

"He did. But she still comes to visit." He slid out of the cab and shut the door, his gaze scanning the outbuildings. "I don't see Bob's four-by-four."

"If you're looking for Daddy, he's gone over to your place." Aleshia floated down the porch steps, graceful as a deer. With her heavy eye makeup, white poet's shirt, ornate necklace, and dangly earrings, she could have been walking down a runway at a fashion show. "He came barreling in a few minutes ago, grabbed his hunting rifle, and took off. Mom went too—she's trying to talk some sense into him."

"You sure he went to my place?"

"Oh, I'm sure. He's looking for Scott. You'd better hope he finds him, because if he doesn't I have a feeling he'll go for the next best target. I called ahead to warn Mary, but no one answered."

"Come on, Jennie." Tom popped back in the truck just as Jennie was getting out.

Jennie wanted to question Aleshia more about Scott but set the intention aside for later.

Aleshia neared the truck. "Oh, hi, Jennie. I didn't realize that was you. Mom said you and Lisa were here. You'll have to come over later and see some of my new designs."

"Sure. I'll mention it to Megan." Jennie thought it odd Aleshia would be so calm when her father was packing a gun and seeking revenge. Jennie would have been worried sick. *Would have been? You* are *worried sick.*

Tom shook his head and shoved the truck into gear, backed around, then headed down the driveway.

"She seems awfully calm." Jennie glanced back. Aleshia was getting into her car.

"Humph. Sometimes that girl has about as much common sense as God gave a goose. 'Course, I suspect she's gotten used to her dad's rages by now."

Jennie didn't comment. Instead, she fixed her gaze on their destination and prayed that no one would get hurt.

Tom stopped at the end of the drive to let a semi pass, then burned rubber as he peeled out onto the main road. Jennie held on to the dash, pressing her feet against the floor. He slowed down to pull into the driveway. A mink ran in front of the truck and narrowly missed becoming another victim.

When they approached the house, Jennie let out the breath she'd been holding. Bob's red pickup was parked in the driveway, right next to Scott's Honda. Through the open window in the cab, she could hear them shouting.

"They're down by the mink barns." Jennie pushed open the door and took off running.

Scott and Mr. Sutherland were just outside the first barn facing off, fists in the air. With Scott's build and youth, she suspected he would win if they actually came to blows.

Christine stood several feet away from the men, holding what must have been her husband's rifle at her side. "Bob, please. Stop this nonsense before someone gets hurt.

"Oh, Tom." She tossed him a pleading look as he and Jennie came alongside her. "I'm so glad you're here. I tried to stop him, but—"

"At least you got the gun away from him." Tom shook his head. "It would serve Bob right if I let Scott beat the pulp out of him."

Mr. Sutherland grumbled something Jennie couldn't hear.

"I didn't release your mink," Scott yelled back.

"Then how do you explain your affiliation with ARM? My daughter told me—"

"I don't care what she told you. I don't even know her."

"You lying scum . . ." Sutherland jabbed at Scott's face. Scott raised his arm to block the punch but didn't swing back.

"Leave him alone, Bob!" Tom tried to get between them. "This isn't going to resolve anything."

"You stay out of this. You should be thanking me. He was about to release your mink too." Sutherland turned back to Scott. "Come on, you coward. You pacifists are all alike." He started swinging, one punch after another.

"I wasn't . . ." Scott blocked all but the last, which landed square on his nose. He staggered back, holding the back of his hand to his face. It came away bloody. He looked at his blood-streaked fist. Scott did strike out then, landing a blow to Sutherland's jaw. The older man staggered backward, slipped in the mud, and landed on his backside.

Sutherland spasmed in pain. "My back—I can't move."

Christine set the gun on the ground and hurried to her husband's side. "I was afraid this would happen." She glanced at Scott. "He has a bad back."

"I'm sorry. I didn't want to hurt him." Scott sniffed and brushed more blood away with his shirt sleeve. "He wouldn't let it go."

"It wasn't your fault," Christine assured him. "But I think you'd better go take care of that nose."

While Tom and Christine helped Sutherland to his feet, Jennie walked with Scott to the house. "I have some tissues in the car."

"I don't need any tissues." He jerked his arm away from her grasp.

"Fine, bleed to death, then." She went to the car anyway, shoved the seat forward, picked up a box of tissues, and rejoined Scott on the steps in front of the old house.

He had blood all over his shirt and hands. Jennie pressed the tissues to his nose. "Tip your head forward and I'll pinch the bridge of your nose. Hopefully that will stop the bleeding."

"I'm sorry," he said, obeying her orders. "I shouldn't have gotten mad at you."

"Shush. Don't try to talk. You can apologize later."

She concentrated on Scott's nose while Tom, Bob, and Christine made their way to the Sutherlands' truck. Bob was walking unassisted now, bent over and limping.

"You should have just let me shoot him, Christine. Tess isn't going to do anything." He shot Jennie and Scott an angry look.

"Bob, for heaven's sake, you're not thinking straight. Did it ever occur to you that Scott might be innocent? Let it go before Tess ends up arresting you. Even if he did have something to do with the release, you know better than to confront them. You're lucky he didn't hurt you worse." She yanked open the driver's side door. "You'd better let me drive."

"I'm holding you responsible for this, Tom." Sutherland grimaced as he stepped up into the cab. "If you hadn't hired him . . ." The car doors slamming and the sound of the truck's engine obliterated the rest of their conversation.

Tom watched them drive away, then came over to where Scott and Jennie were sitting. "How's the nose?"

"I'll live." Scott brushed Jennie's hand away and held the tissue himself.

Concern shadowed Tom's face. "Maybe we should take you in and have a doctor look at it."

Scott shook his head.

"That might not be a bad idea," Jennie agreed. "It's stopped bleeding, but it might be broken. He hit you pretty hard."

"It's been broken before." He stood and started to go inside. "I'll just wash up."

"When you're done, come on over to the shop," Tom said. "We need to talk."

"Yeah, sure." Scott's tone was sarcastic, and Jennie felt like hitting him.

"What are you trying to do, get yourself fired?" Jennie asked when Tom was out of earshot. "You really need to work on your people skills."

"What difference does it make?" Scott stripped off his shirt and went inside. "He's going to fire me anyway."

"How do you know that?"

Scott turned back around to face her. Gripping her shoulders, he searched her face. "Jennie, I . . ." He looked away and dropped his hands to his side. "I was wrong to think you and I could pick up where we left off. Sutherland is right about me. I'm nothing but trouble. You're better off not having me as a friend."

"Scott—"

He held up a hand to silence her. "Just go, okay? And don't get involved with this. There's nothing you can do to help."

"I already am involved. Maybe I can talk to my dad."

"No! You don't get it, do you, Jennie? I don't need your help, so just leave me alone."

"Fine." Jennie took a step back. "If that's what you want."

Pausing in the doorway, she turned back around. "Scott, just answer me one question. Last night I saw someone come into the Bergstroms' yard. Right after Sam fired the rifle off to wake us up. That was you, wasn't it?"

Scott's gaze fell to the floor. "It isn't what you think, Jennie."

Jennie flashed him a disgusted look. "You did it, didn't you? You released the mink, and you lied to me about being affiliated with ARM. You lied to me about knowing Aleshia, too. All this time I've been trying to convince myself and the others that you didn't do it."

Scott looked as if he wanted to cry but didn't say a word. He turned and headed for the bathroom.

"Why?" Jennie's voice caught on the tears lodged in her throat.

He answered only with the responding bang of the bathroom door as it closed behind him.

8

A note on the kitchen table announced that Lisa, Megan, and Mary had gone into town for groceries for the party Megan had planned for Saturday evening.

"Great. This is just great." Jennie sank into the chair, wondering what to do next. She'd planned on telling Tom about Scott's admission of guilt, but he was down at the barns and Jennie didn't feel like looking for him. Instead, she dragged herself over to the wall-mounted phone near the pantry and grabbed the phone book. "I hate to do this, Scott, but . . ." Finding the number, she dialed the sheriff's office.

"You've reached the Linn County sheriff's office. Sheriff Parker can't come to the phone just now. If this is an emergency, please hang up and dial 9–1–1. If you'd like to speak with the sheriff on another matter, leave your name, a brief message, and the time and date you called, and we'll get back to you as soon as possible."

Was it an emergency? She was about to turn her friend in for a serious crime. "Sheriff Parker, this is Jennie McGrady. I have some information on the Sutherland case. Please call me." She checked the Bergtroms' number on the phone and gave it to the machine.

Jennie hung up, feeling miserable and guilty. Why the guilt, she had no idea. She was doing the right thing by turning Scott in and letting the sheriff know he had been the shadowy figure she'd seen. And she felt badly about not warning Tom and Mary about Scott's background. Maybe if she'd said something sooner . . .

No, it wouldn't have made any difference. The plan to release the mink had gone into motion long before she'd come—probably long before Scott had arrived. Still, something didn't feel right. Somewhere in the back of her mind she harbored the notion that Scott couldn't have released those mink—at least not willingly. But he'd admitted his guilt. And why would he lie about a thing like that? It was probably just wishful thinking on her part.

She sighed, knowing she should contact the sheriff immediately—before Scott had a chance to leave the area. At the sound of an engine starting up, Jennie ran to the front porch. "Scott, wait!" She raced down the steps. Scott revved the engine and flipped up the kickstand with his booted foot.

"Don't try to stop me, Jennie. It won't do any good." He put his helmet on and left the strap dangling. "I have to follow this thing through."

"So you're just going to run away?" She stopped just short of him, wishing with all her heart there were something she could do to change the situation.

Scott's jaw was set in anger, his green gaze remorseful. He pulled her into his arms, raised his helmet, and kissed her full on the lips, then let her go. "Now, move—the last thing I want to do is hurt you."

It's too late for that, she felt like saying. "I have a call in to the sheriff," Jennie told him. "I have to tell her."

Scott nodded and bit his lower lip, looking like he wanted to say more.

Jennie stepped away as he slipped the Honda into gear and drove away. "At least fasten your helmet!" she yelled after him. When he reached the end of the driveway, she expected him to turn right and head west toward the freeway. Instead, he made a left—a route that would take him past the Sutherlands' and into town. Strange.

She stood there several minutes, arms folded, staring at the dust until it settled back onto the road and the landscape blurred. She should have jumped on the back of the bike, wrapped her arms around him, and not let go until she'd talked some sense into him. She should have tried to talk him into turning himself in. Jennie debated calling the sheriff again, but something held her back. She didn't want Scott to go to jail, but it was more than that.

He did head into town, she reminded herself. Hope flourished inside her. *Maybe he decided to turn himself in after all.*

Jennie thought seriously about getting into her car and following him but doubted it would do much good. *Let it go, McGrady*, a small voice in her head insisted. *Forget about him. He isn't worth the tears or the trouble.* She shuffled to the porch and sank into the swing wishing she hadn't come to the Bergstroms' at all. It was bad enough having to deal with Ryan's rejection. Now Scott had decided he didn't want her either.

She'd have been better off staying home, working on her project for school, playing catch with her little brother, and hanging out with Mom and Dad. Jennie glanced at her watch. Twelve-thirty. Missing her family brought another rush of tears. She brushed them away and went inside.

Mom had come to depend on Jennie's help the last few weeks. How was she doing without the extra help? Was Dad able to take up some of the slack? Self-pity turned to concern as she picked up the phone.

Calling home produced nothing more than another answering machine message. Jennie hung up. Maybe she'd call later. Maybe not. What could she say? "Hi, Mom and Dad, my new boyfriend—or rather ex-sort-of boyfriend—is an eco-terrorist."

Okay, McGrady, enough. She needed to concentrate on something else. Jennie looked through the cupboards until she found a bag of peppermint tea and a mug. Tea often helped her think things through—Gram had taught her that. After heating the water in the microwave, Jennie snapped up a pen and paper from beside the phone and sat down, imagining herself having a cup with Gram. She thought of Gram's warm smile and deep blue eyes. "What's troubling you, darling?" Gram would say.

Jennie would tell her and together they'd talk it out. Instead of talking, between sips of tea Jennie wrote the details of the story from start to finish. The call from Scott saying he was working on the mink ranch. The talk they'd had and his assurance he was no longer affiliated with ARM. Seeing him in the yard at two A.M. just after the mink had been released. How he'd worked with her and the others to round up the mink and how angry he'd been at the activists who'd freed the animals. And finally, his admission of guilt.

Taking a sip of her now lukewarm brew, Jennie frowned at the paper. It made no sense—no sense whatsoever. Why would he be angry with the activists if he was one of them? Unless, of course, it had all been part of an elaborate scheme to make everyone believe he was innocent. If that was true, she had completely misjudged Scott; that was not a good sign. To be in law enforcement she'd need to be a good judge of character. Though she'd been wrong about people a few times, she still trusted her instincts as well as her intuition. Right now both seemed a bit out of tune.

So what are you going to do about it? The question came as clearly as if Gram herself was sitting at the table.

"Try to find out what's going on, I guess," she said aloud. As Jennie was taking her empty cup to the sink, the phone rang.

"Jennie, this is Sheriff Parker. What have you got for me?"

Jennie told her about the fight and about Scott being the figure she'd seen just after the release and his admission of guilt.

"I appreciate the call. I'll try to track him down. You say he was heading toward town?"

"The last I saw."

"Hmm. Okay, thanks for the info."

"Um—you'll let me know, won't you? I mean, if you find Scott."

"Sure."

Jennie hung up, wondering again why Scott had driven east instead of west. He apparently hadn't gone to town to turn himself in, or Sheriff Parker would have said something.

Had he gone to meet someone?

Jennie's stomach catapulted. Maybe he'd decided to go back to the Sutherlands'. If he did, Jennie would bet just about anything it wouldn't be to apologize. Could Scott have gone to have a showdown with Bob Sutherland? He hadn't even wanted to hit Sutherland during the fight. *How can you be sure?* she asked herself. *Obviously you don't know him as well as you thought.* Or did she? She recalled the way he had angrily lashed out at her and Gram in Florida when he'd been so intent on saving the dolphins. He had a temper—especially when he thought someone was in the wrong. Maybe she'd let her imagination conjure up a Scott that wasn't real.

At the sound of a car coming up the drive, Jennie set her thoughts on hold and went out to the porch to see who it was.

Mary, Megan, and Lisa pulled into the driveway and tumbled out of the car. Jennie ambled out to greet them and helped bring in the groceries.

After making five trips to the car and back, Jennie slumped into a chair. "What are you going to do with all that food?"

"Are you kidding?" Mary laughed. "I'm afraid I won't have enough. I talked to your mom this morning, and they're coming for the barbecue dinner on Monday."

"Mom and Dad are coming too," Lisa added.

"And don't forget the guys are coming over tonight," Megan added.

At Jennie's questioning look, Megan went on to remind her about Algie, Kurt, and Scott.

Jennie winced. With all the excitement, she'd completely forgotten about the party. "Somehow I don't think Scott's going to make it." She went on to give them the details.

"My goodness," Mary exclaimed. "We go shopping and all you-know-what breaks loose."

"This is awful." Megan set two containers of milk in the refrigerator. "Are you sure Scott was in on releasing the mink? It's so hard to believe."

Jennie pointed to the pad she'd been writing on. "Tell me about it. I've been trying to figure it out since he left. Something weird is going on, that's for sure."

"Without Scott," Lisa began, "Jennie won't have a date tonight."

"I don't need one." Jennie bounced to her feet. "I'll stay in Megan's room and read."

"You will not." Megan retrieved a bag from the table and moved it to the counter. "But you're right. We don't need another guy. It's not like a date anyway. We'll just hang out and have a good time."

Jennie bit the inside of her cheek. With Scott in trouble, she didn't feel like hanging out and having fun. But she couldn't very well tell Megan that. Instead, she smiled. "I'm sure it'll be great, Megan. We'll just go with what you've got planned."

"Speaking of plans," Mary said, "weren't you girls going into the English Rose for lunch today?"

The trio glanced up at the clock above the sink. "Oh, you're right." Megan piled some canned goods into the cupboard. "We'd better get ready."

"Shouldn't we help put this stuff away?" Jennie asked.

"Not a problem. You girls go ahead. I can handle the rest."

Jennie reluctantly followed Megan and Lisa upstairs. Ordinarily she'd have enjoyed their outing, but with Scott . . . Jennie cancelled the thought. She was not responsible for him or his actions, and she was not about to let him ruin the rest of her weekend.

While Megan and Lisa talked about what to wear, Jennie pulled her hair out of its braid and began brushing it. "Jeans are okay, aren't they? They're all I brought."

"Sure. I just thought it would be fun to dress up a little. Living on the farm, I'm *always* in jeans." Megan pulled a dress from her closet. "How's this one?"

Jennie eyed the long-sleeved casual cotton dress and shrugged. "Looks good."

"Too good." Lisa rolled her eyes. "I didn't bring a dress. All I have that's even remotely dressy are my black jeans and my lace-trimmed top."

"That's perfect. Lace always dresses up jeans." She eyed the dress and put it back, choosing instead a pair of black slacks and a cable-knit sweater.

While the other girls changed, Jennie rummaged through her suitcase and came up with a lavender ribbed knit. It had a simple scoop neck and looked nice with the gold locket she liked to wear.

Jennie pulled the shirt over her head, tucked it into her jeans, and settled the locket into place, all the while thinking of Scott.

"Are you ready, Jennie?" Megan interrupted her reverie.

"Huh? Oh, sure."

Within minutes they were seated in Jennie's car, Lisa in the front and Megan in back, heading down the long driveway. Jennie studied the road and the traffic, looking for signs of mink as well as for Scott. While she'd vowed to forget him, it wasn't that easy. In the short time she'd known him, she'd gotten quite attached to him. And she was just plain worried.

———————

Tea was an elegant affair, and Jennie had a great time reminiscing with Megan and Lisa, sipping Earl Gray and eating from the three-tiered trays of tiny sandwiches, scones, and desserts.

Megan suddenly stopped talking and leaned toward them. "Guess who just walked in."

Jennie twisted around, then turned back quickly. Aleshia and her mother followed a hostess to a nearby table.

"Oh, Mother, look who's here." Aleshia tossed them a look that could easily be taken as condescending if it hadn't quickly disappeared behind a warm smile.

Christine set her large tapestry handbag on the floor and turned to greet them. "Hi, girls. What a surprise. I needed some time away from the farm. With all the turmoil over the mink, I haven't had a minute to relax, so we decided to meet in town." Her gaze settled on Jennie. "How is your friend's nose?"

Jennie shrugged. "Okay, I guess. Did the sheriff talk to you?"

"Tess? No, is something wrong?"

"I'm afraid your husband was right," Jennie said. "Looks like Scott was involved in the release after all."

Aleshia's eyebrows shot up. "Really? How do you know that?"

Jennie explained again about Scott's confession and at the same time looked for a reaction from Aleshia but saw nothing to indicate that she knew about what Scott was up to. "Guess he must have been a member of ARM all along." Turning to Christine, she said, "I was afraid he might be heading your way."

Christine tucked her hair behind her ear and it bounced back again. "I haven't seen him. But then, I haven't been home. I left to go shopping a few minutes after I dropped Bob off at the house, then came here."

"How's his back?" Jennie asked. "Looked like he was in pretty bad shape when you left."

"I suspect he'll end up going to a chiropractor in a day or two. Tried to talk him into letting me take him to the doctor, but he said he had too much to do at the farm." She shook her head. "Men."

A phone rang and Christine leaned over to retrieve her handbag. Digging out and unfolding a cellular phone, she pressed a button and said, "Hello?"

The lines on her forehead deepened as she listened to the caller. Aleshia, Jennie, Megan, and Lisa fell silent. The feeling that something was wrong came back to Jennie with twice the impact it had before. She twisted her napkin and listened intently.

"I don't understand. He must be there somewhere." Christine's questioning gaze flew to Aleshia. "Did you check the barns?" She hesitated for a response, then said, "I don't know what to say, Tess. If his truck is there, he's got to be. Unless—did you check with Tom? Maybe his back got worse and he asked Tom or someone to take him in." Another pause. "I see." Christine licked her lips. "I'm sure there's a reasonable explanation." As she spoke, Christine set her napkin on the table and stood. "I'll be there in about ten minutes."

"Is something wrong?" Aleshia asked.

"I don't know. That was Tess. She went by to check on Bob and—he's not there."

Aleshia shrugged. "Well, I'm sure there's nothing to be concerned about. Maybe he went for a walk in the woods or down by the lake to cool off."

"Let's hope so." Christine shoved her chair in and headed for the door. Jennie strained to hear the last part of the conversation.

"Tess suspects foul play. His tractor is in the lake."

"In the lake? But Daddy would never . . ." Aleshia shoved open the door and stepped outside.

9

"You don't need to come," Mary said after explaining that she was heading over to the Sutherlands'. Bob Sutherland still hadn't been found, and Mary felt she needed to be with Christine and Aleshia to lend support if necessary. "And it's possible they'll need help with a search."

"I'd like to go," Jennie said. "I've had first-aid training. Maybe I can help."

"Me too," Megan and Lisa said together.

"You'd better change first. It's getting cold and wet out there." A storm front had moved in, dropping the temperature by about ten degrees. While it wasn't exactly raining, the sky hung heavy with clouds that managed to drench everything with a fine mist.

Mary waited while the girls hurried upstairs to change into warmer, more casual clothes. Jennie pulled a green University of Oregon sweat shirt over her top.

"I still can't believe this." Lisa gathered up her long red curls and wrapped a scrunchie around her ponytail. Loose tendrils sprang back around her face. "Feels like we're in some kind of weird dream."

"Sure does." Megan tossed her brush on the dresser and began digging through one of the drawers. Underwear, bras, and socks went flying.

"What are you looking for?" Jennie asked.

"Socks. We should wear boots," Megan said. "I have lots of extra heavy ones you can borrow." She tossed out several white crew socks and three pairs of thick gray-and-red woolen ones. Following her lead, Lisa and Jennie tugged on two pairs of socks and headed downstairs and donned jackets, rain slickers, and rubber boots.

Five minutes later, the foursome walked along the path at the lake's edge. They would eventually end up on the other side where Sheriff Parker, two men in scuba gear, Jim Owens, and Tom stood on the bank waiting for the tow truck operator and another man to attach the hook to the back of the tractor and haul it out. The narrow ramp that slanted down to the lake was lined with vehicles.

"They've already done some diving." Mary stooped to pick up a blade of grass, then twirled it around in her hand as they walked. "They found a pair of Bob's gloves in the water and are afraid he might be trapped under the vehicle."

"Couldn't they have been on the tractor?" Jennie asked.

"Yes, but as Tom pointed out, neither the tractor nor the gloves would have been down there without Bob or one of his hired hands. And at this point he's the only one missing."

Jennie shuddered. "Does the sheriff think he was murdered?"

"It's a possibility, but she's looking at other options too."

"Like?" Megan reached down to pet the bassett hound.

"It could have been an accident. Bob may have been working on the irrigation system. He pipes water to the mink barns from the lake. There are a number of possibilities, including the fact that he may not be there at all."

"Then how did the tractor get into the lake?" Lisa asked.

"Your guess is as good as mine. Maybe they'll have some answers for us." She nodded to the group at the lake's edge.

In the few minutes it took to walk around the lake to where the rescue operation was going on, the tow truck driver had nearly accomplished his task. The tractor emerged from the water, muddy and dripping with algae.

Jennie stood back with the others, ten feet or so from the water. She closed her eyes and bit into her lower lip, praying Sutherland's body wouldn't be pulled up with it. She didn't want him to be dead and imagined him walking up to the group demanding to know what they were doing on his property.

The tow truck's engine geared down to idle. Water running from the tractor sounded like a dozen miniature waterfalls. For several long moments no one spoke. Jennie opened her eyes and along with the rest let her gaze drift over the water's surface. They watched in a funeral silence as the ripples settled.

"What now?" the tow truck driver asked.

"We send the divers in again." Tess began inspecting the tractor, most likely looking for evidence to explain why it had gone into the water. Jennie moved closer to the vehicle. It was a small tractor, similar to the one she'd driven at Tom's when she helped feed the mink. The key was still in the ignition in the on position. With the front facing the lake and the gearshift in drive, it looked like someone had purposely driven it into the water.

Her first thought was of Scott. Could he have done it for revenge? She could imagine Scott being mad enough to run the tractor into the lake, but if he had done it, where was Mr. Sutherland? Come to think of it, where was Stan? Jennie glanced around but saw no sign of him. Maybe he had something to do with Sutherland's disappearance.

"Um, Sheriff, I was wondering about the man who works for the Sutherlands. I don't see him. Could he have taken Mr. Sutherland somewhere?"

Tess gave her an it's-none-of-your-business look, then said, "He's the one who called me. Stan got a call from his brother. Apparently Stan's mother was injured in an accident of some sort, and Stan had to go to Portland to see her."

How convenient, Jennie mused. With his wife and daughter both gone, that left Mr. Sutherland alone. The scenario sounded like a setup, and Jennie wondered if Tess had thought of that possibility. Maybe she'd ask later. The question was, who wanted to get Sutherland alone? Maybe the same one or ones who released his mink. *Maybe Scott.* Jennie quickly shoved the thought aside.

Tess checked out the tractor and told them exactly what Jennie had surmised.

"Is all this really necessary?" Aleshia stared into the murky water. "I mean, he can't be in there. He doesn't swim—" As if the foolishness of her comment occurred to her, she flushed. "I mean . . . he probably got mad at the tractor and drove it in here himself, then stalked off somewhere to work off his anger. You know how he does."

"That's not likely, Aleshia." Jim Owens moved to her side and took her into his arms. "Your father has always been careful with his equipment."

Aleshia rested her head on Jim's chest. "Then why?" She leaned back to look at him. "It wasn't supposed to happen like this."

Jennie did a double take. She wasn't the only one.

Jim stepped back and gripped Aleshia's arms. "What do you mean? You're not saying . . . You told me you didn't have anything to do with the release."

"I didn't." She struggled to escape his grasp. "Let go of me."

"Then tell me what's going on." Jim dropped his hands to his sides.

Tess had perked up as well. "Yes, Aleshia, I think that might be a good idea. Did you know about the release beforehand?"

"Aleshia?" Christine started toward her daughter, then stopped.

"It's all right, Mom." Aleshia tossed her mother a sad look and rubbed her upper arms. "I had no idea they were going to hit my parents. It's just that I understand how ARM operates and this isn't the way they work. They cut through the fences, release the animals, and clear out. It's too dangerous to hang around. Her gaze drifted to the ground. "Besides, they're my friends. They wouldn't have hurt my family."

Tess eyed Aleshia with interest. As a law officer she'd be taking in every detail, suspecting everyone—even family. Aleshia would be a primary suspect, but not the only one. One by one, she'd talk to them all, find out where they were, and what, if any, motive they had. Jennie hoped to question them all as well, in her own way. She tried to determine whether or not Aleshia was telling the truth but could never make eye contact with her. If body language had anything to do with it, Aleshia was lying, or at least she wasn't telling them everything she knew.

Christine wrapped her shawl more tightly around herself. She still wore the gauzy autumn-colored dress she'd had on at the restaurant. Her lips had turned a corpse-like shade of blue. "M-maybe we should go up to the house to wait."

Jennie wasn't sure who she'd issued the invitation to, but she didn't want to leave, not yet.

Aleshia stared at the water again. "You go if you want. I'll stay here."

Christine nodded. "How about you, Mary? Do you and the girls want something warm to drink? It's getting so cold."

Mary nodded. "Yes, that might be a good idea. Girls?"

Jennie opted to stay, hoping she'd find out more information. Lisa and Megan said they'd get the hot chocolate and bring some back for the others. Jennie turned up the collar of her jacket and inched closer to the water to get a better view of the divers.

Fifteen minutes passed before the thermoses of hot chocolate and coffee came. Megan and Lisa poured everyone a cup, ending with Jennie.

"Find anything?" Lisa handed her a steaming cup.

"Thanks." Jennie shook her head. "Nothing yet."

"Megan and I are going back over to the house to get stuff ready for tonight. Are you staying long?"

"I'm not sure." She took a sip of the hot drink. "I'd like to at least stay until they finish diving."

Lisa leaned forward and whispered, "You're worried that Scott had something to do with Mr. Sutherland's disappearance, aren't you?"

Jennie glanced up and noticed Tess watching them. "Scott wouldn't kill anyone." She spoke loud enough for Tess to hear.

"Everyone is capable of murder, Jennie." Tess moved over to where they were standing. "Even your friend."

"I . . . I know. But . . ." She sighed. "Never mind." How could she tell the sheriff she had a feeling about it? It wasn't anything she could explain. She just knew.

When Lisa and Megan left, Jennie took her cocoa to the Adirondack chairs where Aleshia was sitting. The four wooden lawn chairs sat in a half-moon around a fire pit and faced the lake. On a clear day the view would have been breathtaking. Today it was dismal and depressing. Fog and low clouds closed off the view and dampened everything around them, including their spirits. After repeated efforts Jim finally got a fire going.

"Are you going to be okay?" he asked, hunkering down in front of Aleshia.

Her gaze moved from the water to his face. "Sure. You go ahead."

"We'll find him, honey." He stood, leaned over to kiss her, then walked up the road.

Jennie stood as near to the fire as she dared, staring at the flames and listening to the sizzling sound of raindrops hitting the hot logs. She wanted to talk to Aleshia, ask questions, but didn't know where to start.

"Where's he going?" Jennie finally asked.

For a moment Jennie didn't think Aleshia heard or hadn't wanted to. She looked at Jennie as though she were seeing through her. "To the mink barns. Said he wanted to go through them more thoroughly. There are a lot of places to hide a body in there."

Jennie swallowed hard, surprised at the callousness of the statement. "That's a gruesome thought." She moved to the empty chair at Aleshia's right and dropped into it.

"This entire operation is gruesome and premature if you ask me. I don't think my father is dead, but everyone else seems to. Maybe I'm kidding myself. You know what they say about denial being one of the first stages of grief."

Jennie looked in the direction Jim had gone, wondering why he went alone. She thought about following him when one of the divers emerged waving a hammer.

"Found it partly buried a few feet from where the tractor went in."

Tess examined it and brought it over to Aleshia for identification.

"It might be Dad's." She looked ready to crumple. "He kept one like it in his tool belt in the shop."

"We'll save it as evidence." Tess made some notes in a small notebook and stuffed it back in her shirt pocket.

Aleshia stood. "I could be mistaken. There are a lot of hammers like that one, aren't there? I should go up to the shop and see if Dad's is missing."

"Good idea," Tess said. "Jennie, why don't you go with her? It will give you both something to do. Don't touch anything, just look. You don't need to come back down here. I'll come up to the house as soon as we're finished."

Jennie didn't comment but fell into step beside Aleshia.

"I get the distinct impression she was trying to get rid of us."

"Yeah. I'm glad for the diversion, though."

They walked several yards before Aleshia spoke again. "She wants you to keep an eye on me."

"What makes you say that?" Jennie frowned, sensing the same thing.

"If I'm alone I could put a replacement hammer in Dad's tool belt. That is, if he's missing. Like it or not, Jennie, you're coming along as a witness."

"Maybe she wants us to keep an eye on each other." Jennie dug her hands deep in her pockets as a gust of wind seemed to blow right through her. "We're all suspects at this point."

"True. But you have no motive. I do. You see, Jennie, Daddy threatened to cut me out of his will if I didn't cut my ties with ARM. Money is a primary motive, isn't it?"

Jennie digested this new piece of information, amazed Aleshia would offer it. It occurred to Jennie that accompanying Aleshia might not have been a good idea. Not that she especially feared Aleshia. But Jim was somewhere in the mink barns supposedly searching. What if they had been working together? She imagined herself walking into an ambush. Jim could be waiting. Jennie reigned in her imagination. *Don't be ridiculous,* she told herself. *Neither of them would gain anything by hurting you.*

Jennie stopped just outside the shop door. "Did you do it?"

Aleshia pushed the wide metal door about two feet to the side—barely enough space for them to slip through. "You apparently don't think so. Neither does Tess. Otherwise why would she send you with me? And why would you have come?"

Jennie's heart quickened. She watched her warm breath turn to a puff of smoke when it hit the cold air. Maybe her imagination wasn't that far off. What was Aleshia up to? Where was Jim?

Aleshia's lips curved in a malevolent smile. "Not a smart move, was it? If I headed the release and killed my father, what's to stop me from killing you too?"

10

Jennie could tell Aleshia was having fun at her expense but wasn't quite ready to trust her.

Aleshia chuckled. "Aren't you coming in?"

When Jennie didn't move, Aleshia pushed the door open wider. "I was teasing. I'm not going to hurt you."

Jennie gritted her teeth. "You're not funny. Pretending you're the bad guy could get you into trouble."

"Who's going to know?" Her smile faded. "I'm sorry, Jennie, but you looked so serious."

"It's a serious matter."

"You're right. I shouldn't be joking about Dad's disappearance, but like I said, I don't want to believe there's anything to it. You know what the Bible says about laughter being good medicine. It reduces stress." She sighed. "Well, I've stalled long enough. Let's go see if we can find Daddy's tool belt."

Even though she didn't think Aleshia would hurt her, Jennie cautiously stepped into the shop, letting her gaze drift over the machinery, the tables, and up to the open rafters. She saw no sign of Jim or anyone else. The shop was neatly arranged. Tools of every sort hung from hooks that had been set into pegboards or screwed into the beams. Equipment—another tractor, a flatbed trailer, and a three-wheeler—sat in a row of stalls, ready for use. A pegboard next to the stalls held keys and were neatly labeled. One set of keys above the label "Tractor B" were gone—still in the ignition. A place for everything and everything in its place.

"Whew. One thing's for sure," Jennie said, "you could never

accuse your dad of being messy."

"Daddy was in the marines. He's compulsive when it comes to keeping his work area neat. It's his way or no way."

She relaxed some and followed Aleshia to a center post. The tool belt hung on a four-inch-long nail.

"The hammer isn't here," Aleshia said, obeying Tess's order not to touch it. "But then, I guess I didn't expect it to be."

"I thought I heard someone out here." Jim's voice echoed in the building like an explosion. Jennie's feet nearly left the ground.

"Jim." Aleshia ran to him, threw her arms around his neck, and started crying. Her action startled him, but he recovered quickly, wrapping his arms around her. "What's going on?" He soothed his fiancée's hair, but his accusing gaze settled on Jennie.

When Aleshia didn't answer, Jennie cleared her throat. "The divers found Mr. Sutherland's hammer in the lake near the tractor. We came up to check his tool belt."

"I keep hoping he's okay," Aleshia sobbed. "It just keeps getting worse."

"I'll admit things aren't looking too good, but let's not panic yet." Jim took hold of her shoulders and leaned back to look at her. "Why don't you go up to the house? Keep your mom company."

"No . . . I . . ."

"Don't argue. I'll let you know everything that happens."

Aleshia hauled in a deep breath, and Jennie expected her to tell him off for ordering her around. Instead, she kissed him and said, "All right. Mom must be frantic."

"I'll walk you up to the house." He settled a protective arm around her shoulers and started for the door.

"What kind of power does he hold over you?" Jennie wanted to ask but didn't.

"Do you want to come in too, Jennie?" Aleshia paused at the opening.

"No . . . um . . . you two go ahead. I'll go tell Tess about the tool belt."

Aleshia nodded and they stepped outside.

"Just a minute," Jennie heard him say a moment later. "I need to give Jennie a message for Tess. Keep walking, I'll catch up."

Jim came back in. Fear reared up inside her. She needed to stop being so paranoid.

He gave her an odd look, then said, "I went back through all the buildings. Didn't see any sign of Bob, but I got to wondering about something."

"What?"

"Come back in here and I'll show you."

Jennie ignored the warning bells and followed him. There was no need to be nervous. Jim wouldn't try anything with Tess only a few hundred yards away. Still, she followed at a safe distance, watching, waiting for him to make a move.

Jim led her into a large room that looked like a lab. It was set up a lot like the one Tom used for skinning the mink and preparing pelts. But where Tom's worktables were wooden and rustic, Bob's were cabinets covered with white Formica. Only the Formica wasn't all white. Blood was spattered over one of the counters.

"Take a look at this, Jennie. It's probably from the mink—usually we don't get much blood. Once in a while, though, we might hit an artery."

Jennie felt queasy. "You said it was probably mink blood."

"Yeah—that's what I thought earlier. Now I'm wondering if it might be Bob's. He'd never leave a mess like this. He was a stickler for cleaning up after himself. This probably means someone interrupted him and—well, I just think Tess needs to see this."

"Hasn't she been in here?"

"No, Tom and I looked for Bob up here and then checked around the grounds—that's when we found the tractor. Tess has been concentrating in that area." He glanced nervously behind him. "I'd better get back to Aleshia."

"Um—sure, but could you answer one question?"

"If I can." His frown deepened.

"Tess said Stan called her about Mr. Sutherland. Why were you looking for him?"

"Tom came over to check on him—see if he needed help. Couldn't find him and got worried. Stan told him he'd called the sheriff. He took off, and Tom called me to help look for him."

Jennie nodded.

"Look, if you think Tom or I had anything to do with Bob's

disappearance, you're way off base."

Jennie shrugged. "What I think doesn't matter."

"No, I don't suppose it does." He looked worried, frowning as he took a step back, then turned.

Jennie took a few deep, settling breaths. She moved closer to the blood-spattered counter. Jim was right. The sheriff would be very interested in determining whether or not the blood was human. The mystery was unfolding minute by minute, drawing Jennie in. She knew she wouldn't be able to rest until the truth was brought to light. There were so many questions—so many unknowns. Jennie left the shop, closed the door behind her, and jogged back to the lake. Only Tom, Tess, the two divers, and the tow truck driver remained. She met Tom halfway up the ramp and told him about the tool belt and her conversation with Jim.

He shook his head. "Situation keeps getting worse."

"Are you going?" Jennie asked.

"Yep. Can't stand around doing nothing. Thought I'd go back to the farm and get some work done. Tess knows where to find me. You're welcome to come with."

"That's okay. I need to tell Tess about the blood in the shop. I'll see you later."

She'd just finished reporting the possible evidence to Tess when the divers emerged for the final time. So far all they'd found besides the tractor was a hammer and gloves. This time, too, they came up empty-handed.

"He's not down there," one of them said, stripping off his mask and hood. "Lake's not all that big or deep through here, and we've thoroughly covered this portion. We could go out farther, but unless someone took a boat out and dumped him in the middle, I doubt we'd find him. There's no current so he wouldn't have drifted."

Jennie released a sigh and picked up the empty mug she'd set on the arm of one of the Adirondack chairs earlier. If Sutherland wasn't in the lake, he could still be alive somewhere. Her mind drifted back to the gloves, the submerged tractor, the hammer, and the bloody counter in the shed. She had the gut feeling all was not right with Sutherland, but as long as they didn't find a body, she'd hold to the hope that he would show up feisty as ever.

"Thanks, guys. Appreciate the help," Tess said.

"Anytime," the second one answered.

Tess ran a hand through her short curls. "If he is in there, it's too late to help him. We'll do a land search and hope we have better luck."

"What's the plan at this point?" The diver bent to pull off his flippers.

"We'll keep looking," Tess said. "I have a Search and Rescue team coming with a couple dogs. If he's here, they'll sniff him out. I need to check out the shed for evidence of foul play. Could use your help up there as well."

"You got it. We'll change out of these wet suits, dry off, and see you up there."

When the divers had gone, Tess asked the tow truck operator to haul the tractor into Albany, where they could have a forensics team go over it. In the meantime, she planned to check over the shed, take samples of the blood evidence, and tape off the shed as a possible crime scene.

Jennie walked with Tess to her squad car. "Do you think the tractor was a diversion? I mean, the divers didn't find the body in the lake. Could the tractor have been driven in there to throw us off the real trail?"

Tess smiled as though she found Jennie's comment amusing. "Maybe."

"You think ARM is responsible?"

"Aleshia's right about the MO. Before when ARM has conducted a release, it's been get in and get out. They don't usually come back. I'm not saying it didn't happen."

"They could have decided to change the way they work," Jennie offered. "What if they kidnapped him and are holding him hostage?"

"Not much point in that. However, they may have killed him to send a message." She opened the passenger side door and set the gloves and hammer, which she'd bagged, in the back. "There's one thing about that scenario that puzzles me, though. If ARM is responsible for Sutherland's disappearance, why haven't they owned up to it?"

"Maybe it's too soon."

"Would you like a ride to the house?"

"Sure." Jennie ducked inside and automatically fastened her seat belt, then waited for Tess to climb in. Like most police vehicles, the car was fully equipped with a radar scanner, a rifle, radio, and all types of other paraphernalia. Tess picked up the radio and started the car at the same time. She backed around and headed up to the main driveway. The call was to a dispatcher to check on the progress of the Search and Rescue team.

"Should be there in another fifteen minutes," the gravelly voice said.

"I'll be waiting." Tess replaced the mike and turned to look at Jennie. "You're wondering about your boyfriend again, aren't you? You worried he might be involved in Sutherland's disappearance?"

"I—I don't know. Anyway, he's not my boyfriend. I told you before. . . ."

"Yeah, yeah—just a friend. If it's any consolation, I've got the state police looking for him. He won't get far."

That wasn't what Jennie wanted to hear. She felt totally confused and at odds with herself over Scott's guilt or innocence. As much as she wanted to believe in him, part of her couldn't help but question his motives for coming to the mink farm in the first place. *Why are you doing this to yourself, McGrady?* He admitted he'd been in on the raid. Sutherland bloodied his nose, and she had seen him head toward the Sutherland farm when he left.

"Hey, you did the right thing calling me."

"It sure doesn't feel right."

"Having a friend involved in criminal activity is always hard. Thing is, if you don't go to the police, you're helping them escape, and that's a crime. It's like saying you agree with what they're doing."

"I know. I just wish I could see him and talk to him. I feel so lousy not knowing for sure—about Scott and Mr. Sutherland, I mean. We don't even know for sure if Mr. Sutherland is missing."

"True. Ordinarily I wouldn't even be looking for him yet. Usually we wait twenty-four hours, but with the tractor and the fact that he was in that altercation with your friend—we needed to move on it. Now I have a hammer that may have been a murder weapon and possible blood evidence. We may be chasing our tails here but"—she shrugged—"what can you do? If it were my husband I'd want someone on it yesterday."

Husband. Somehow Jennie hadn't associated Tess with a husband, but of course she'd have one. Jennie remembered the picture of the little boy on her desk.

"What does your husband do?"

"Ex—" She pulled into the driveway behind several cars and turned off the engine. "Paul is an engineer for Boeing in Seattle. Cinderella story gone bad. The prince didn't like the idea of my being a cop. He tolerated it as long as I stayed in Seattle. When the position opened down here and I suggested the move—well, let's just say he took advantage of the opportunity to divorce me. End of story." She offered Jennie a wan smile. "I get my little boy on holidays and an occasional weekend. The judge didn't think my career was stable enough to warrant full custody. He also felt I should be home instead of out chasing criminals." She looked down at the steering wheel and shook her head. "More than you ever wanted to know, right?"

Among the twangs of bitterness, Jennie detected a still-broken heart. Tess must be incredibly sad. "I bet you miss him."

"Yeah, I do." She pinched her lips together and pulled the key out of the ignition. "I haven't told anyone that in a long while. You'd make a good cop, Jennie. You're the kind of person people open up to. Comes in handy."

"My folks have had some trouble," Jennie admitted. "Dad used to work for the DEA. Mom didn't like his being an agent. He was missing for five years, and everyone thought he was dead. Mom got a divorce so she could marry someone else. But then Dad came back. I don't think she would have remarried him if he'd stayed with the DEA. They compromised. He's still a police officer, but Mom is handling it better now. She still doesn't want me to be a cop, though, but we compromised there too. I'm going to get a degree in law. Maybe someday your husband will come around."

"That's doubtful. I don't plan on giving up my job." She hauled in a deep breath. "Speaking of which, I'd better get back to it."

Jennie went with Tess to the shop to show her what she'd seen. "That's funny," Jennie said as they approached the building. The door had been opened. "I closed the door when I came out."

"Maybe Jim came back in," Tess suggested. "Let's go see."

"I can't believe it." Jennie eyed the nail that Mr. Sutherland's tool belt had been hanging from. "The tool belt is gone."

Tess grunted. "Looks like Mr. Sutherland is back, or else someone is removing evidence."

The strong scent of Pine Sol drew Jennie to the area where she'd seen the blood. Someone had cleaned up the mess.

"The plot thickens." Tess folded her arms.

"You can still tell the blood was there, can't you?"

"Probably, but I doubt we'll be able to determine whether it was human or animal."

Jennie felt sick. The attempt to destroy evidence pretty much proved a crime had been committed. And that crime was probably murder. She shuddered at the thought that a killer could have been standing on the very spot she was now. *Stop it, McGrady. You don't know there was a murder. Okay, it looks like something happened to Mr. Sutherland, but like you told Tess, it could have been abduction.*

After Tess was through looking around, they headed up to the house. Mary let them in and settled them both at the table with coffee for Tess and tea for Jennie. Tess reported what they'd learned so far and wanted to know if Aleshia or Christine had been out in the shop.

Mary gasped and leaned forward, holding her cup in both hands. "You're not suggesting they destroyed the evidence, are you?"

"Not knowingly. Could be they felt the need to clean things up. Grief works on people in different ways."

"Well, neither of them have been outside. Christine took a sedative when she came in and has been upstairs sleeping for the last hour. Jim brought Aleshia in and she's sitting in the living room in front of the fireplace, right where he put her. Poor thing is beside herself. I imagine she feels guilty. If something has happened to Bob, she'll never have a chance to make amends. It's always hard to lose a parent, but when the relationship is as volatile as the one Aleshia and Bob had, it's doubly hard."

"What about Jim?" Jennie asked. "Did you see where he went after he brought Aleshia in?"

"No. He just said he had to get back to work. I assumed that meant he was going to our place."

Since Jim was the one who talked to her about the bloody counter in the first place, she doubted he'd go through the trouble of cleaning it up. But who else could have?

She couldn't think. The tea was making her warm and sleepy. She propped her elbows on the table and rested her chin on her hands, trying to place the various people who might have had access to the shop after she'd been there. The list included everyone except Tess, the divers, and the tow truck operator.

"You look exhausted, Jennie. Why don't you let me drive you back to our place and you can take a nap?" Mary asked.

Jennie yawned. "I am tired, but I don't want to miss anything. Besides, I want to help."

"There's nothing you can do right now." Tess set down her cup.

"I could go out with the Search and Rescue team."

"I don't think so. It's possible that whoever destroyed the evidence is responsible for whatever happened to Bob. That means they're still around and could be armed and dangerous. I have backup coming in, and we'll do another search of the barns. Go home, Jennie, where you'll be safe."

"All right. I could use a nap."

Mary stood. "I'll take you, then come back. I feel I should stay around."

"You don't have to drive me. I'll walk."

Reluctantly, Jennie slipped her coat back on and stumbled to the door. She said her good-byes to Tess and asked them to let her know of any news. She didn't want to give up, but at this point, like Tess said, there wasn't all that much she could do.

Jennie set out on the path along the lake. About halfway around she stopped. Had she heard something? The cool air brought her wide awake. Being near the lake had jump-started her adrenaline. Or maybe it was the rustling she heard in the bushes not ten feet away.

11

Panic turned Jennie's legs to rubber. Her heart pounded. She should run, but her feet refused to move. There it was again. One thing was for certain, she was no longer alone. The tall grass to her right shuffled and waved.

Just about the time Jennie was going to take off screaming, Drooley lumbered out, carrying something furry in his jowls.

"Drooley, what have you got there? Put it down."

Drooley gazed up at her with big, sad eyes, then whimpered and obediently dropped the furry creature at her feet as if that had been his purpose all along.

Jennie recognized it immediately as one of the missing mink. "Good boy." She had first thought the animal dead, but when she knelt to examine it, she realized it was still breathing. She didn't especially want to pick up the mink for fear it would bite her. Finding a stick, she prodded at it. The fur on the underside of the neck was bloody and matted. Jennie unzipped her jacket, scooped the small animal up, and settled it in a sling she'd made by lifting up the bottom of her sweat shirt. "Let's get this guy home, Drooley. Maybe we can still save him."

Drooley ran ahead, nose to the ground, snooping in the bushes and grassy clumps along the way.

Several vehicles out on the main road slowed down and turned into the Sutherlands' driveway. Search and Rescue, no doubt. She thought of going back but figured she'd only be in the way. And she did need to rest up for Megan's party. She doubted she'd have much fun, but Megan and Lisa had worked so hard, it wouldn't

76

be right to back out. Besides, they wouldn't let her.

The Search and Rescue unit would concentrate their search in the woods that began near the house and extended over to the Bergstrom farm on one side and down to the road on the other. Woods that Jennie was walking parallel to that very moment. Tess was right. The evidence she'd gathered spelled foul play, and whoever had tampered with the evidence could still be out there. She quickened her steps but didn't run so as not to jar the small patient nestled against her tummy.

Rather than stop at the house, Jennie went straight to the barns where she thought Tom or Jim would be. She found Tom hosing down some empty pens.

"Hey, Jennie." Tom turned off the hose when he saw her. "Any word about Bob?"

"Still haven't found him. They'll be combing the woods with dogs about now. Someone washed the blood off the counter." Though Jennie didn't really suspect Tom, she watched his face for signs of surprise or guilt nonetheless.

"Now, why would anyone want to do that? Unless . . ." A worried look replaced the frown. "Someone seems to be toying with us, don't you think? Could be the folks from ARM are aiming to strike again. On the other hand, it doesn't seem like they'd want to draw attention to themselves. This is mighty strange. Tess tell you what she thinks about it?"

"She's puzzled." Jennie gently unfolded her sweat shirt and lifted the small mink out of its warm cocoon.

"What have we got here?"

"Drooley found him. He's got a cut on his neck." Jennie handed the animal to Tom. "Don't know if Drooley hurt him or just found him like that."

Tom examined the little critter and began walking toward the machine shed. "My guess is the latter. Drooley's been trained to hunt down mink and bring them to us. You remember how helpful he was after the release at Bob's. He treats them like a mama would her babies."

Drooley snuffled and barked at the sound of his name. He sat on his haunches, gazing up at the creature he'd rescued. He looked expectantly from Jennie to Tom, then barked again.

Tom reached down to pet him. "Think you deserve a treat for this one? Well, I do too. Jennie, how about getting a biscuit out of that container in the corner while I see to our little friend here."

Jennie made a production out of giving Drooley his treat. He licked her hands and face in appreciation. When he'd finished scarfing it down, they went back to watch Tom. He carefully cleansed the wound, which had stopped bleeding, then placed the animal in a small cage. "Would you like me to take it over to the Sutherlands'?"

"Not yet. We'll keep an eye on her tonight and see how she's doing in the morning. If she makes it, I'll let you do the honors. We'll keep it up at the house tonight where it's nice and warm. I'll mix up a protein drink." He took a can of powdered mix down from the shelf above the workbench and scooped a small amount into a plastic container, added water, and handed the mix to Jennie. "If you'd like, I'll let you take her to the house. Give her to Mary or Megan. They'll know what to do."

"Sure." Jennie took the food in one hand and the caged mink in the other.

She and Drooley left Tom to his chores and headed up to the house. Going past the older house where Scott had stayed, a wave of disappointment washed over her. "Oh, Scott," she murmured. "Why did you have to get involved with ARM? We could have had so much fun together." She sighed and shifted her gaze to Drooley. "Guess all we can do now is pray for him, huh?"

Lisa and Megan met her at the door eager to hear about Mr. Sutherland. Drooley nudged his way in. His toenails clicked on the entry floor as he made his way to his water dish.

Jennie handed off the mink to Megan and told them about Drooley's heroic rescue. Taking off her jacket, she stepped into the kitchen and inhaled the pungently delicious scent of barbecued chicken and ribs. "Mmm—that smells so good. I'm starved."

"So were we. We've been grazing on veggies." Lisa nodded toward the fresh vegetable platter on the counter. While she brought them up to date, Jennie washed her hands and began munching on a celery stick.

"I feel terrible about Mr. Sutherland." Megan set the cage on the floor in the corner of the kitchen by the heating vent. "I hope they find him soon. One way or the other, it's better knowing."

"That's for sure." Lisa hunkered down beside the cage. "What can I do to help?"

"We'll have to put it up on blocks and set paper under it." Megan went into the porch and rustled through a stack of papers. "Mink have this unique way of going to the bathroom. They designate one area of the cage for their messes. That's why you see those little piles under the cages." She meticulously laid out several sheets of newspaper on the linoleum, then set two bricks in the center of the paper, parallel to one another and about a foot apart. She picked up the cage and balanced it across the two bricks. "She'll be okay here."

"Oh look," Lisa squealed. "Its eyes are open. Maybe it's saying thank you."

Jennie laughed. "Could be."

Drooley, his big belly nearly brushing the floor, almost tripped over his feet getting to the cage.

"Slow down, boy." Megan chuckled and petted him. "Silly thing. You gonna take care of your guest?" She looked up at Jennie. "Don't worry. Drooley thinks it's his job to guard over strays. Whenever we have an injured animal—and living out here, we've had plenty—he sits with them. Hardly leaves their side until they're well." She rubbed his back. "Don't you, boy? That's a good puppy. Yes, you are."

Jennie smiled at Megan's baby talk. Drooley loved it. "He's a great dog."

"The best, aren't you, Drooley."

Megan sat back on her heels, pressed her hands to her thighs, and looked up at the digital clock on the microwave. "I don't want to rush you, Jennie, but the guys will be here any minute."

"Are you still planning to eat down by the lake?"

"No. Algie says there's another storm coming through. He suggested we go into town to a movie after we eat and go in the hot tub when we get back."

"What's playing?"

"*Free Willie*. I know it's old, but our movie theater never shows anything but older movies. If we want new ones, we have to go into Lebanon or Salem."

"I love that movie. Reminds me of Scott." The words were out before she had a chance to catch them.

"I'm sorry, Jennie." Lisa's empathetic look nearly brought tears to her eyes.

"It's okay. Um—he didn't call or anything, did he?"

"Scott? No." Megan offered her a tight smile. "I can still ask Algie to bring another guy. . . ."

"Don't do that." Jennie recovered quickly. "I don't need a date. I just need to know Scott is okay."

"He will be," Lisa assured. "We just need to have faith."

"Right." Jennie clamped her lips together, grabbed a couple of carrot sticks, and headed for the stairs. "I'm going to take a shower. See you in a few minutes."

Jennie took the stairs two at a time. In spite of the tragic aura the day's events had cast over her, she was looking forward to the diversion. Food, a movie, and a hot tub sounded wonderful. In the shower, she relished the warm spray of water, imagining it washing away the griminess outside and the worry within. Whatever Scott had gotten himself into was no concern of hers, and she had to stop worrying about him—at least for a few hours.

When she'd finished showering, Jennie blow-dried her hair and dressed in clean jeans, a white T-shirt, and a black crocheted vest. She picked up the pad she'd taken notes on earlier and jotted down a brief description of the day's events and listed the clues. Nothing made much sense, but writing it all down would help her remember the details later.

Hearing a vehicle crunch to a stop in the driveway, Jennie set her pad aside and peered out the window. Two guys jumped out of a shiny plum-colored truck with turquoise scrollwork and a forest scene on the side. The wheels came up to the driver's waist. It had a rack of lights on top of the long four-door cab. The driver, Algie, Jennie guessed, reminded her of a telephone pole with arms. The other, Kyle, was almost as tall but stockier. Lisa would definitely not be disappointed. "If you aren't interested, Cuz," she mumbled to herself, "maybe I will be."

"Jennie, they're here," Megan yelled up the stairs.

"Coming." She hustled down the stairs, eager to meet her companions for the evening.

Kyle's grin practically reached his ears when Megan introduced him to Jennie.

"This is so cool. I saw you on television—on that missing person's show. You were trying to find your dad."

Jennie winced. "That was probably the biggest mistake I ever made. My dad didn't want to be found."

"You mean he ran away from home?"

"No. He was an undercover agent with the DEA working on a major drug case. He had to change his identity to protect us, and I blew his cover. But everything worked out okay."

Lisa lifted her heavy mop of golden red curls off her neck and let them fall back again. "She's been in the news a lot lately. Jennie has solved nearly as many cases as the police this year."

"She exaggerates." Jennie tossed Lisa a put-a-sock-in-it look.

"Well, you have, Jen. And I have a feeling you're going to solve this one too."

"You mean the release at the Sutherlands'?" A frown etched Algie's features. "You don't want to get involved with those guys, Jennie."

"I'm not involved, but thanks for the warning. I don't want to believe Scott could have anything to do with this whole mess, but he doesn't seem to have much of an alibi."

"You really care about him, don't you?" Megan looked at Jennie as if she knew exactly what she was going through.

"Yes, but I feel like an idiot for letting him get to me the way he did. Um . . . can we talk about something else?"

"Sure, dinner's getting cold anyway," Megan said.

"Then let's eat." Kyle grinned first at Jennie, then Lisa, extending both arms. "Ladies? May I escort you to the table?"

"Why, I'd be delighted." Lisa took one arm, Jennie the other.

Dinner was as good as it smelled. The light banter went on between the five of them all through their meal. Kyle and Algie entertained them with stories of their summer adventures, which included several raft rides on the Rogue River and hiking around Crater Lake.

"I love the woods," Lisa said after they'd told them about their near escape from a bear who'd invaded their camp. "The last time Jennie and I went hiking, Jennie got shot at and fell into the Lewis

River. Went right over a waterfall."

"And you're alive to tell about it?"

Jennie eagerly added her story to the growing collection of tales. "We were crossing the river on a log when a bullet hit it. I had some first-aid supplies in my backpack. God must have sent a guardian angel to protect me because instead of landing on the rocks, I fell into a deep pool behind the falls. I managed to climb onto a rock, but I nearly froze to death. For a while I thought I was trapped in the cavern. I finally decided it was either die there or try to make it out. I managed to find a way back through at the side of the falls where the force of the water wasn't so great."

"She got life-flighted into Portland," Lisa added.

"Sounds like you lead an exciting life, Jennie." Kyle sent her a look of pure admiration.

Jennie's lips curled in a reflective smile. "I guess I have." *And it isn't nearly over yet,* she mused. As much as she wanted to forget Scott and enjoy the evening, she couldn't stop the overwhelming notion that something even worse was about to happen.

After dinner they piled into the truck, the two guys in front and the three girls in back. Algie's truck was loaded with amenities including a state-of-the-art CD player, which he cranked up to ear-splitting volume, a radar scanner, and a cell phone. The one thing it didn't have was good shocks. They bounced along the lonely stretch of road into Thompson, which luckily was only seven miles away.

Once inside the theater, Kyle settled himself between Jennie and Lisa. Megan sat next to Lisa, and Algie grabbed the end spot on the aisle. Jennie watched the movie with bittersweet memories. It so reminded her of Dolphin Playland and of Scott. The hero's love of the whale touched her deeply. Seeing the whale soar over the boy and on to freedom at the end just about broke her heart. Scott was so much like the young boy Jesse. A chip on his shoulder and a big heart. Tears blurred the screen. *Oh, Scott, what's happened?* Jennie knew in her heart that Scott hadn't hurt Mr. Sutherland. She doubted he'd released the mink, but if he hadn't done it, then why . . .

Kyle took hold of her hand, drawing her out of her reverie. He gave her a look of compassion as though he understood what she was thinking. She wouldn't tell him she hadn't been crying about the movie. She just smiled at him and pulled her hand away to dig a tissue out of her pocket.

Try as she might, Jennie couldn't recapture the light mood she'd been in earlier. A strange quiet seemed to have settled over all of them. Maybe they were just winding down. They piled into the truck again for the trip home. Lisa closed her eyes and tipped her head back against the seat. Jennie rested her elbows on her knees in the cramped quarters and stared out the window. The road was dark and lonely. Most of the clouds had dissipated, giving way to a sliver of a moon and a bazillion stars. Algie clicked on his brights, lighting up the roadway. A flash of light off the side of the road brought Jennie up short. "Wait!"

Algie slammed on the brakes. "What—"

Lisa jumped "What's wrong? You scared me half to death!"

"I saw something—back there. A reflection."

"It's probably a can or a piece of aluminum foil or something." Algie inched ahead.

"You think we should check it out?" Kyle asked.

Jennie felt foolish. She had no idea why the flash seemed so important, only that it did. "It might be nothing, but I'd like to go back and look."

"Okay." Algie slipped the truck into reverse and moved back several feet. He hit the switch on the searchlights on the top of the cab. "We'll be able to see better with these."

Kyle got out and opened the door for Jennie.

She took his hand and jumped to the ground. Her gaze scanned the roadside, coming to rest on a wrecked motorcycle some thirty feet off the road in the wide ditch. It was partly submerged in the shallow water.

Kyle must have seen it too. "That rearview mirror must be what caused the reflection you saw, Jennie."

Jennie didn't answer. All she could do was stare in horror at the bike she now knew to be Scott's and the body that lay beside it.

12

Jennie mentally climbed out of the rockslide of emotions that had just dumped themselves all over her. *You can't fall apart now, McGrady. He needs you.* This was not just Scott, but an accident victim. "Get an ambulance!" she managed to shout while she rushed ahead of the others. Algie was already punching the numbers in on his cell phone.

"Scott!" Crouching down beside him, she yelled his name again and shook him. No response. She bit hard into her lower lip, forcing herself to place her fingers on the side of his neck to feel for a pulse. "Come on, Scott, please don't be dead."

She couldn't find a pulse. "I need more light!" she shouted. "Do you have a flashlight or something?" Placing her hand to his mouth, she thought she detected a faint breath.

"Hang on, I'll turn the truck at an angle." The engine roared to life, and Algie aimed the searchlights at them.

Scott was lying prone, dried blood on his face and hands. His helmet lay beside him intact. Maybe he'd taken it off or forgotten to fasten it. But she couldn't think about that. She forced the random thoughts out of her head and concentrated on what she needed to do. She unzipped his jacket and placed her ear to his chest. Detecting a heartbeat, she released the breath she'd been holding. Jennie glanced up at the others. "He's alive. Thank you, God." Jennie continued to check him for injuries. His skin felt cool and clammy, and he still wasn't moving. Blinking back tears, she struggled to stay calm. His leg stuck out at an odd angle.

"Looks like his leg's broken," Kyle commented.

Jennie had already surmised as much. She shrugged off her jacket and draped it over him.

"Maybe Al and I could put him in the cab where it's warm." Kyle hunkered down beside her.

"No. It's too risky to move him."

"She's right. Here, this might help." Algie handed her a silver emergency blanket. "We keep a first-aid kit in the back of the truck," he explained.

"Thanks." She left her own jacket in place and wrapped the silver blanket around Scott as best she could.

"Ambulance is on the way. Shouldn't be too long."

"I take it this is the guy who was supposed to hang out with us tonight?" Kyle took his jacket off and put it around Jennie's shoulders.

Jennie huddled under it, thankful for the warmth. The jacket was almost as comforting as a pair of arms might have been.

"No wonder the sheriff couldn't find him," Lisa said. "Do you think he's been out here very long?"

"Hard to say." Algie shivered and stuffed his hands into his pockets. "The ditch is deep, and with the brush and grass he'd be easy to miss. If Jennie hadn't caught sight of the reflection . . ."

Jennie shuddered at the thought. Moisture from the cold, damp ground seeped into her jeans at the knees. "You guys should wait in the car. No sense all of us freezing our buns off."

"No way," Lisa said.

"We're here for the duration, Jennie," Kyle agreed.

They stood in a half circle around Jennie and Scott, shielding them. Tears filled her eyes and trickled down her cheeks.

Moments later she heard the sirens—saw the flashing lights. She brushed away her tears and greeted the rescuers with a concise report on Scott's condition—just as she'd been trained to do.

In a matter of minutes the paramedics had Scott stabilized and loaded in the back of the ambulance. Jennie insisted on riding along. She wanted to be there if—no, *when* he woke up.

Lisa gave her a hug. "We'll follow you to the hospital. Um— do you want us to stop and pick up your car? That way if the guys want to leave . . ."

"Sure." Jennie dug her keys out of her backpack and handed

them to Lisa. "Just be careful with it."

"I will." Lisa hugged her again. "He'll be all right, Jen. I know he will."

"Yeah. I hope so." Jennie climbed in beside the paramedic and Scott.

Kyle settled an arm around Lisa's shoulders and steered her in the direction of Algie's truck. *Nice guy*, Jennie thought. They both were. Megan was lucky to have them as friends.

The doors closed and they were off—sirens blaring. The others went to pick up Jennie's car, then met her at the hospital. There they waited in the emergency room. There wasn't much to say. Jennie gave Kyle back his jacket and settled in a chair in the corner. She was barely aware of the conversation between Lisa, Kyle, Megan, and Algie. The girls were bringing them up-to-date on Scott's supposed involvement in the case. Jennie didn't want to speculate. All she wanted was for Scott to be okay.

Sheriff Parker came in thirty minutes later and headed straight for Jennie. "Heard we had a hit-and-run."

"Looks that way."

"How is he?" The sheriff's face was tight and drawn—like she'd been on a couple of all-nighters.

"Aside from having a broken leg and a concussion, I'm not sure. The doctor is still with him."

"Sorry I couldn't get here sooner. Had another release up north. Been out there for the last two hours."

"Another one?" Megan groaned. "When is it gonna stop?"

"It probably won't—not as long as there are fur farmers and animal rights activists." Tess lowered herself into the chair, settled her right leg on her left knee, and began to massage her ankle.

"Who was it?" Algie asked.

"The Caseys. They're about twenty miles west of here. Small operation. Eight thousand or so mink. Family business. The owner's son got beaten pretty badly, but he was able to give us a good description of the guy who beat him."

"At least we know it wasn't Scott."

"Well, we don't know for sure. The hit was around four this afternoon. You found Chambers on the road west of here, around nine-thirty, right?"

"They released the mink in daylight?" Megan asked.

"The owners are out of town for the weekend. We have a neighbor trying to get ahold of them. He's keeping an eye on the place in the meantime and has hired a guard."

The doctor Jennie had spoken to earlier ambled into the waiting room, his scrubs stained with blood. "Ms. McGrady?"

Jennie stood. "Finally. Can I see him?"

"For a few minutes."

"Is he awake?"

"Drifts in and out. We need to get him casted, then we'll put him in a room. I'd like to keep him overnight. If everything checks out, he can go home in the morning."

"I'd like to see him first." Tess was on her feet, all official again. "Need to ask him some questions."

Jennie bristled. "You're not going to arrest him, are you? I mean—with all he's been through. It's not like he's going anywhere."

"Relax, Jennie. I'm not a tyrant. He may have some pertinent information on Mr. Sutherland and more important, whoever hit him. I'll talk to him tonight. The arrest, if I make it, can wait until morning."

"Can I go with you while you question him?"

Tess smiled. "You really like this guy, don't you?"

"I . . . he's a friend. I told you that."

Tess gave her a knowing smile. "Sure. But much as I'd love your company, I need to talk to him alone. I won't be long."

Tess followed the doctor into the emergency room, and Jennie paced back over to the water cooler, poured herself a cup, swallowed it in two swigs, and tossed the cup in the trash. The wait was excruciating. Not only was Jennie anxious to see for herself that Scott was okay, she was also curious. What had happened to him? Had he gone to see Mr. Sutherland? Who had run into him? What was going on? The circumstances surrounding this case were getting more and more bizarre.

While sitting with him alongside the road, Jennie had made a decision. She believed in Scott and knew that if he had helped with the release it had been for a good reason. She took a deep breath.

You'll find out soon enough. The door to the emergency room opened and Tess came out.

"He's asking for you, Jennie."

"Thanks. Did you learn anything—about the hit-and-run?"

"No. It was dark—around seven. Said all he saw were the headlights."

"Do you think someone hit him on purpose?"

"Looks that way."

"But why?"

"When we find the driver, we'll find the answer to that one. For now, all we can do is examine the evidence." Tess turned Jennie toward the emergency room. "You go on in there and hold his hand. Leave the investigation to me."

Jennie nodded and went through the double doors. The room was like any other ER in a small rural hospital, three or four patients tucked behind partially closed curtains, medical personnel hustling from one place to another. There were about six cubicles. Scott was in the one at the far end of the room. For some odd reason, Jennie's heart thumped heavily inside her chest, and her palms were sweating. She felt like a performer with a severe case of stage fright and took several deep breaths to calm herself down while she walked the wide hallway. The curtain was open so she gingerly stepped inside. A lab tech was drawing Scott's blood.

"Hi." The word squeaked past the lump in her throat.

Scott turned his head to look at her and stretched out his left arm. Jennie stepped up to the stretcher and took his hand. " 'Bout time you showed up, McGrady." He closed his eyes, wincing as the needle punctured his skin.

"I'll be done in a minute." The tech released the tourniquet and dropped it in her tray. After drawing three vials of blood, she pressed gauze to the injection site and withdrew the needle. Placing tape across it, she instructed him to hold it tightly for a minute or so until the blood had a chance to clot.

When she'd gone, Jennie turned her full attention to Scott. "You look terrible."

A smile brightened his craggy features. "Thanks a bunch."

"What's the deal, Scott? What's going on? You wanted me to believe you were involved, but I know you didn't release those mink, and I know you didn't harm Mr. Sutherland."

"I thought I could handle it, Jen. But ARM is just too powerful."

"What do you mean? What happened to Mr. Sutherland?"

"You're as bad as the sheriff, you know that?" Scott shifted, groaning and tipping his head back in pain. Through gritted teeth he said, "Like I told her, I don't know anything about Sutherland. I haven't seen him."

Jennie wanted more answers, but he was in so much pain she didn't have the heart to ask. "It's okay." She brushed his dark hair from his forehead. "I'm sorry. Here your leg is broken, you've got a concussion, and I'm interrogating you."

"It's all right." He gripped her hand. "I'll tell you all I know later."

A young man in pale green scrubs approached the bed. "I'm sorry, miss, but I'll have to ask you to step out. We need to get this guy's leg reset and casted. He should be admitted in his room in about an hour."

"Sure." Jennie turned back to Scott. "I'll be here."

Going back out to the waiting room, Jennie gave the others a report, then insisted they go home. She had her car and would stay awhile longer.

"Are you sure you don't want us to wait with you, Jen?" Lisa handed Jennie her keys. "If the others don't want to, I can."

"No, that's okay. You go ahead. The doctor said Scott would be okay. I promised to stick around until his leg is set." Jennie stuffed the keys in her jeans pocket.

"You look exhausted," Lisa said. "Why don't you get some sleep and come back in the morning?"

She was tired. It had been a grueling day, but she had no intention of leaving. "I'll stretch out on the couch in here and take a nap."

"All right." Lisa shrugged into her jacket. "But call us if there's a problem or anything."

"I will." She gave Lisa and Megan hugs and thanked Kyle and Algie for their help.

When they'd gone, Jennie curled her long body onto the short couch and closed her eyes. About an hour later one of the nurses woke her. It took several seconds before she could orient herself to where she was and what she was doing there.

"Sorry to interrupt your sleep, but I thought you'd like to know your friend's room number. We'll be taking him up in a few minutes."

Jennie mumbled a groggy thank-you, and after using the rest room and splashing her face with cold water, she dragged herself down the hall and into room 26. Thankfully, it was a small hospital. In her present condition, anything bigger and she'd probably have gotten lost.

"You must be Jennie." One of the nurses intercepted her in the hall outside Scott's intended room. She had chocolate brown eyes and a wide, cheery smile. Jennie wondered how anyone could look so wide awake at one in the morning. "I'm Crystal Chavez and I'll be taking care of your friend."

"Hi. Um—they told me he'd be here soon. Is it okay if I wait in the room?"

"Sure. How long will you be staying?"

"I don't know."

"Well, you can stay as long as you'd like. There's a recliner in the room if you need it. The last patient was a little boy. We had the chair moved in for his mom so she could spend the night. Not the most comfortable bed, but it's better than a straight-back chair."

"Sounds fine to me."

"Oh." Crystal turned in the direction of the voices and the two green-garbed men wheeling a stretcher toward them. "That must be Scott now. Why don't you let us get him settled, then you can go in."

Jennie backed out of the way while they wheeled Scott in. He'd apparently had to go to surgery to get his leg set because he was wearing one of those silly shower caps. His dark curls peaked out from under it. His thigh-high cast rested on pillows. Ice packs lay over the cast to keep the swelling down. He was asleep—probably still under from the medication they had given him. His handsome face looked like an impressionistic painting with all its bruises. She suspected the black eyes were from the broken nose Mr. Sutherland had given him. The others—the abrasion on his chin and the swelling along his jaw—must have been from the accident.

Jennie wandered to the end of the hall and back. Peeking in the room she saw that they'd transferred him to the bed and were getting ready to leave. She waited until they'd taken out the stretcher before going in. Crystal wrapped a blood pressure cuff around his arm, and after checking that and his pulse and respirations, she wrote them down on the chart. She then checked the IV site and solution and explained how to work the call light. "I'll look in on him every few minutes, but if you need anything, just push the button."

Jennie nodded, then stood beside the bed a long time, wishing she could read Scott's mind but not getting a clue as to what had happened to him that day. What had he meant about ARM being too powerful? Had they coerced him into working for them?

His eyes slowly opened. They looked dazed and unseeing. His lips curled in a half smile. "You're still here."

"I told you I would be." She took hold of his hand when he reached for her.

"Shouldn't have left like I did this morning."

"It's okay, you don't need to talk now. Plenty of time for that later."

"No . . . need to tell you in case something happens to me." He seemed to forget what he was saying, and the next words out of his mouth were "I love you."

Jennie swallowed hard, not knowing how to respond. She cared a lot about Scott, but love? As a friend, sure, but . . .

"Don't want you to get hurt."

"I don't understand."

"No accident. Be careful." His eyes drifted closed again. "Need to stay away from me . . . or they'll get you too."

"Who'll get me?" Jennie tightened her grip on his hand.

"Don't know—too close."

"Shh. Just rest, Scott. You're safe here."

"Water."

He's delirious, Jennie told herself. *He doesn't know what he's saying.* Still, he might be trying to tell her something important. Jennie offered him a drink from the glass on the bedside stand, placing the straw between his dry lips. "Who are you talking about?"

Scott opened his eyes, their green depths hazy. He raised his head slightly, sucked in a couple of swallows, then let his head fall back onto the pillow without answering.

It was still too soon to ask. Jennie chastised herself for being so persistent. He needed to rest. Morning would be soon enough to talk to him.

"How's our patient?" Crystal came in and handed Jennie a blue cotton blanket. "In case you decide to go to sleep. It can get chilly in here at night."

"Thanks. He woke up for a minute—talked but didn't make much sense. I gave him some water. Hope that was okay."

"That's fine. I wouldn't expect him to be making too much sense at this point." She checked his vital signs again.

"Can I get you something—tea or a cold drink?"

"Tea would be nice."

She nodded. "Be right back."

Crystal came back a few minutes later and set the tea on the bedside stand. Making one last check on her patient, she left.

Jennie settled into the recliner and drank the soothing chamomile tea. It felt good and warm. She tucked the blanket around herself, reclined the chair, and watched Scott. The tea relaxed her, and in moments, unable to keep her eyes open, she set the cup on the floor beside her and drifted off to sleep.

"Excuse me, Jennie? Wake up. It's morning."

Jennie groaned, wondering whose voice had entered her dream. It was a woman's voice, but not Mom's. And not Aunt Kate's or Gram's. But then, it wouldn't be any of them. She wasn't home. And this wasn't her bed. It wasn't a bed at all. Little by little the events of the night before tumbled into her head. Scott. She opened her eyes. An older woman in a pastel uniform smiled down at her. "Sorry to wake you, dear, but we have a patient coming."

"Patient?" Jennie frowned at the odd remark and glanced at her watch. Eight o'clock. "I didn't mean to sleep so long. How's. . . ?" Jennie's question hung unfinished as her gaze settled on the empty bed.

13

Jennie rubbed her eyes and looked at the bed again. Her eyes weren't focusing—probably from lack of sleep. "What happened? Is he . . ." She couldn't bear to say the word *dead*. But that didn't stop her mind from racing on with the thought. "He was all right last night."

"Who was, dear?" The older nurse looked at Jennie as though she had two heads.

"My friend Scott. Your patient. He was here last night." Jennie closed her eyes and massaged her temples.

"I'm afraid you must be mistaken. We don't have a patient named Scott."

"Then why am I here?"

"I don't know. Crystal said you were visiting a patient and needed to sleep for a couple of hours."

"What do you mean you don't know? He couldn't have just walked out of here."

The nurse looked uncomfortable. "You seem confused. Perhaps you should see one of the doctors."

"I don't need a doctor."

"I wish I could be of more help, but I really don't know what you're talking about."

"Crystal would know. She's the nurse who was taking care of him. Can I talk to her?"

"I'm afraid not. She's gone home. If she admitted a patient to this room, I'm certain she'd have mentioned it in the report."

Jennie took a deep breath. *Stay calm, McGrady. There has to be a reasonable explanation.* If she could just get her brain functioning. "Okay," she said. "Let's try this again. Scott Chambers was the victim of a hit-and-run. I found him in the ditch and rode in the ambulance with him to this hospital. He saw Dr. Engstrom in the ER, had his leg reset and casted, and was brought up here. Crystal came in to check on him several times."

"Perhaps he was discharged and she forgot to tell me. We had a busy night last night. Several patients to admit. Sometimes patients come in and out so quickly. . . ."

Jennie rubbed her neck—wishing she could get over the strange, woozy feeling. Lack of sleep had left her feeling groggy and nauseated. "He wouldn't have left without telling me." *Or would he?* He'd been concerned for her safety, but he was in no condition to walk anywhere.

"If he was discharged, there'd be a record or a file, wouldn't there?" Jennie asked.

"Of course, but—"

"Please, Mrs. Casey," Jennie read the name on her pin. "I'm afraid something terrible has happened to him."

"All right. We can have a look, but I'm sure you're mistaken." She led Jennie down the hall and into the nurses' office, where she looked through a stack of charts. She shook her head. "Let me try the computer. If he was admitted . . ." She didn't finish the sentence but typed Scott's name and hit enter.

After trying several variations, she looked up at Jennie. "I'm sorry. I have no record of a Scott Chambers ever being in this hospital. I don't know what to tell you."

"How I can get ahold of Crystal?"

Mrs. Casey rubbed the back of her neck. "I'll call her."

The nurse went into another room and picked up the phone. Jennie glanced through the names on the charts, but none of them bore Scott's name. She was beginning to think she'd dreamed up the entire episode. Jennie leaned against the counter. There was no way Scott could have recuperated that quickly—or walked out of the hospital without help. But who would have taken him? Tess? Was it possible she'd arrested him and hauled him off to jail while Jennie was asleep? Doubtful. Make that impossible. She couldn't have slept that soundly. Could she?

"Crystal must not be home. Or else her phone is unplugged. She does that sometimes so the ringer won't wake her up during the day."

"Could you tell me where she lives?"

"No." She wagged her head from side to side. "It isn't that I don't want to help you find your Mr. Chambers, but I can't be giving out personal information about my nurses."

There was no point in arguing. About the only way anyone could have gotten Scott out without Jennie knowing was to have drugged her, and considering the way she felt at the moment, that was certainly a possibility.

She was still groggy but managed to drive the three blocks from the hospital to the sheriff's office.

"Jennie, you look awful. What happened?" Tess asked.

"Scott's gone. The hospital has no record of him being there."

"What? That's impossible. I asked one of my volunteer deputies to keep an eye on him. He'd have told me if . . ."

Jennie gripped the desk. Her knees buckled at the same time her stomach lurched.

"Maybe you'd better sit down." Tess shoved her chair back and came around to the other side of the desk.

"I don't need to sit." Jennie dragged a hand through her disheveled hair, nearly falling in the process. "I just need to know where Scott is."

"We'll get to that in a minute. Now, sit." Cupping Jennie's elbow, she directed her to a chair.

Jennie sank into it and gasped for air. "I don't feel so good."

"Put your head down." Tess pushed Jennie's head to her knees. "Stay put. I'll get a cool cloth."

Within a few minutes the dizziness passed. Jennie sat up and used the cool, wet cloth to wash her face. "What's going on, Jennie? Are you on something?"

"No. I don't do drugs. I don't even take . . . unless . . ." Jennie tossed the cloth on the corner of the desk. "That nurse—Crystal—gave me some tea. I fell asleep right after, and when I woke up Scott was gone. We have to do something. He tried to warn me. Whoever hit him must have come back and kidnapped him from the hospital."

"Stop, Jennie. Do you have any idea what you're saying?" Tess pinched the bridge of her nose.

"I know it sounds crazy, but how do you explain it? He's gone, and if you didn't take him, who did?"

"There's only one way to clear this up. I'll call the deputy. I'm sure it's all a misunderstanding."

Jennie doubted it but didn't say so. Tess would find out soon enough.

Tess picked up the phone and dialed. A frown etched her forehead. "He's not answering." She slid the phone back in its cradle. "Come on." She grabbed her jacket from the coatrack and waited for Jennie to join her. "We're going back to the hospital. I want a doctor to take a look at you. Then I intend to find some answers."

Jennie rode in the squad car, her head resting against the seat. She had no doubt now that there'd been something in the tea. Whatever it was seemed to be wearing off, but not quickly enough to suit her.

Tess picked up her radio and called in her location and her plan to go to the hospital. "Has Jeff checked in with you?"

"No."

"Try finding him for me, will you? And keep trying until you get him."

"Will do."

Jennie's eyelids closed. Not having the strength to open them, she folded her arms and rested her head against the seat.

"Any word on Sutherland?" Tess asked dispatch.

"Nothing. S and R went out at dawn. They haven't reported in."

"Keep me posted."

"Roger."

"Oh, and call Agent Tucker for me. Have him meet me at the hospital. Tell him his decoy is missing."

Decoy? Jennie's eyes snapped open. "*Agent* Tucker? As in FBI?"

"Do you know him?"

Jennie shook her head. "Is the FBI involved?"

"ARM is a national organization. The Feds are conducting their own investigation. Bottom line is they want the head honcho."

"Sonja."

Tess tossed her a questioning look. "How did you know that?"

"Scott told me the first day I was here. It's a code name."

"Agent Tucker may want to talk to you. If Scott really is missing, as you seem to think, he'll be none to happy."

"You said decoy. Was Scott working with the Feds?"

"I really can't disclose anything, Jennie. Tucker made it clear that it was strictly a need-to-know situation."

"Well, I need to know. Was the FBI using Scott to get information about ARM?" It made perfect sense. Scott's anger about the release even though he'd been a part of it—or at least pretended to be.

"You'll have to talk to Agent Tucker. I just learned about the connection this morning."

Jennie nodded. "I can see why the FBI might want to use Scott to infiltrate ARM. He's been a member and might be privy to inside information. With his friend being killed, he'd be willing to help the authorities." Jennie hated where her thoughts were heading. "Someone from ARM must have caught on to Scott's deception. If that's the case, Scott could already be dead."

"You're getting ahead of yourself, Jennie. If ARM wanted Scott dead, why would they go through all the trouble of taking him out of the hospital? There is one other possibility. Agent Tucker may have realized Scott's life was in danger and transferred him to a safer location."

"You think?" She relaxed a bit then, giving in to the hope that Scott was indeed safe and in the protection of government agents. The clandestine flavor of removing any trace of Scott definitely sounded like something the government might do. They may have sworn the deputy and the night nurse to secrecy. Yes, that was it. Scott was one of the good guys. And he was safe.

Jennie held on to that hope during her examination and blood test, which would confirm their suspicions that she had been drugged. Jennie thanked the doctor and walked to the waiting room where Tess was talking to a middle-aged man in a suit. The concerned look on their faces turned Jennie's stomach to mush.

"Jennie, this is Agent Tucker with the FBI. I'm afraid the news isn't good. They don't have Scott. And I still haven't been able to locate my deputy."

"What about Crystal Chavez—the nurse?"

"Nothing so far on her."

"Tess tells me you're a friend of Scott's." Agent Tucker met Jennie's gaze and held it.

"Looks like you were right the first time," Tess said.

"ARM has him?"

Tucker uttered a non-committal "Humph."

"Please tell me what's going on." Jennie wrapped her arms around herself. Scott was in terrible danger and could already be dead.

"Not here." Agent Tucker took her elbow and led her out the door and into his car. Tess followed in her own car. Once they were inside the unmarked vehicle, Tucker slipped the key into the ignition and put the car in drive.

"Where are we going?"

"Back to the sheriff's office. We'll have more privacy there."

Tucker had a wide forehead and gray-green eyes. His hair was a mix of ash-blond, white, and gray. Jennie studied his profile and the stubborn, no-nonsense set of his jaw. "Do you work out of the Portland office?" she asked.

"Yes. And, yes, I know your grandparents and your father. They've advised me to level with you on Scott's involvement so you won't decide to investigate on your own. I'm hoping you'll be able to help us."

Help them? Jennie held in her excitement, wondering what he had in mind. Would they let her infiltrate the group in Scott's place?

Once they were inside, Agent Tucker closed the door, pulled the empty chair around beside Jennie, and set his briefcase on the desk. Sheriff Parker sat behind her desk, arms resting on its surface.

"What I'm about to tell you is strictly confidential." He opened his case but didn't remove anything.

Jennie nodded. "I know how to keep secrets."

"So I've heard." He tossed her a knowing look that Jennie found a bit disconcerting.

She wondered just how much the agent knew about her. *He is FBI*, she reminded herself. *And he knows Dad, Gram, and J.B.*

"Scott came to us several weeks ago," Tucker went on, "with valuable information on a number of key people in ARM. He volunteered to rejoin the organization as a mole and assured us that he would like nothing better than to find Sonja. We have evidence to substantiate our suspicions that ARM's head people have been operating out of the area. Unfortunately, if they discovered Scott's alliance with us, that could already have changed."

"So you set Scott up at the Bergstroms'." So much for fate bringing them together.

"We did that for two reasons."

"Let me guess. Tom Bergstom lives next door to Aleshia Sutherland, who happens to be an outspoken member of ARM, and the Bergstroms are friends of my family."

"Actually, J.B. made the suggestion. We didn't know at the time that Chambers was your boyfriend. Otherwise we might have done things a bit differently. As it turned out, his affiliation with you might have been what fouled things up."

Jennie didn't know whether to defend herself or cry.

"Come on, Tucker, lighten up." Tess gave him a harsh look. "Jennie feels bad enough without having you dump guilt on her for what's happened to Scott. Besides, I happen to disagree. I think Scott saw something or was getting too close. This Sonja or someone else from ARM figured out who he was and what he was up to and ran him down. When they realized they hadn't killed him on the road, they came back to the hospital to finish the job."

"Maybe he told the wrong person who he was," Jennie said. "Or maybe I was too quick to defend him." She tried to remember who she'd talked to about Scott. Tom, Mary, Megan, and Lisa. Had she said anything to Jim, Aleshia, or Christine? Mr. Sutherland?

Jennie snapped her fingers. "I just had an idea. I know it sounds farfetched, but . . . well, suppose Mr. Sutherland is Sonja."

"Farfetched doesn't begin to describe that one." Tess tossed her an incredulous smile.

Agent Tucker frowned. "Now, hang on. I'd like to hear the kid's thoughts on this. Go on, Jennie."

"Suppose he is Sonja. I mean—it is a code name, and Scott said it could be a man or a woman. Sutherland could have had his people release the mink from his farm to take suspicion off himself. I know it sounds weird, but what better cover for a covert operation than to be a fur farmer? And he does seem to be missing. He also spent a lot of time with Scott. Scott could have inadvertently said something that clued Sutherland in. Then Mr. Sutherland could have set up all that evidence himself. Maybe he's lying low for a while." Jennie paused, trying to assemble another piece of the puzzle. Aleshia.

As if reading Jennie's mind, Tess asked, "But didn't he kick his daughter out because she wouldn't renounce her membership in ARM?"

"That could have been for show." Jennie leaned forward, glad she was finally on to something plausible. "You saw how shaken up Aleshia was over her father's disappearance. Even though he kicked her out, there's still a strong bond between them. Could be they're not so different in their thinking after all."

"You may have something there." Tucker smiled. "Good thinking."

He pulled a file out of his briefcase and set it on the desk. "I'd like Jennie to look at these photos. Then I'm going to head over to the Sutherland place. I want you to come with me, Tess. Introduce me as an agent you brought in to help with the case."

"You need a search warrant?"

"Not yet, but we might want to get one just in case. I'd like to have a talk with Mrs. Sutherland and Aleshia. Oh, and the guy Sutherland fired—Jim Owens." He opened the folder and drew out a manila envelope. From that he took a number of black-and-white photos. "Jennie, I want you to look through these and see if you recognize anyone."

Jennie looked at the first one, a shot taken of a crowd of demonstrators holding signs and marching in front of a shop called Furs Galore. "This was taken in Carmel. We've blown up portions so we can see the faces more clearly. Do you recognize any of them?"

Tucker showed her several more sets. Jennie shook her head. On the fifth one she was about to respond negatively when her gaze captured a familiar face. She'd only seen the woman once, and that had been in Florida in front of the Dolphin Playland. "This one," Jennie pointed her out. "It's Melissa, Scott's friend from Florida." Jennie explained their brief encounter. "Back in

May she was picketing at the Playland. She wanted Scott to get information for her about the operation at Dolphin Island, but he refused. Is she a member of ARM?"

Tucker showed her a close-up of Melissa. "This was taken in Portland, when Preston Delacorte appeared at a women's fair to show off his new line of furs. Naturally, ARM was there to protest. It was one of their milder demonstrations. They got him in the face with a raspberry pie."

"Guess their protest worked on him," Tess said. "I heard he decided not to use real furs in his garments anymore."

"Right, and guess who's consulting with him about using her fakes in his fall line."

"Aleshia?" Jennie looked from one to the other.

"Hmm. Now take a look at this one." He shuffled through several and pulled one up. Melissa was holding a protest sign again. An angry-looking man she'd seen in a couple of the other photos flanked her right. On her left stood Aleshia Sutherland.

"They know each other." The implications sent Jennie's heart into overdrive. "Scott told me he didn't think he'd ever met Aleshia, but she knew him. I thought he must have lied to me, but now it makes perfect sense. Scott knew Melissa and might have told her why he was leaving ARM. If Melissa found out Scott was here, she could have told Aleshia about him, and Aleshia told her father."

Jennie stared at the photos. "You knew about Scott and Melissa. He must have identified her."

"Yes. He called Melissa and told her he wanted to rejoin. She was enthusiastic about it, but now I'm wondering if she suspected his motives all along."

Jennie shook her head to clear it. There were just too many puzzle pieces. "What do we do now?"

14

Agent Tucker gathered the photos and stuffed them back in the envelope, settled the folder in his case, and snapped it shut. "Tess and I will question the Sutherlands and Jim Owens. You can go back to the Bergstroms' and forget we had this conversation."

"But—what about Scott?"

"We're as concerned about Scott as you are. We'll find him. I have agents looking into his disappearance right now. I'll let you know as soon as we find anything."

Several minutes later, after Agent Tucker and Tess dropped her off at the hospital so she could get her car, Jennie was intent on driving back to the farm as she'd been told. Her head felt like someone had used it to pound nails into cement. All she really wanted to do was find a quiet place to sleep. Now, if she could convince her mind to cooperate, she'd be fine, but she couldn't get Scott out of her head. "God, please let them find Scott alive."

What worried Jennie was that both Tess and the FBI agent seemed more concerned with capturing the head of ARM than finding Scott. *Let it go, McGrady. Tucker said he had agents working on it.*

Easier said than done. She couldn't stop thinking about the nurse who'd so sweetly given her tea. It had relaxed her all right. Laid her out cold. Had Crystal been an innocent bystander or an accomplice?

Jennie glanced down at her near-empty gas gauge and pulled into a station on the outskirts of town. While waiting for the attendant to fill the tank, she used the rest room to wash her face and comb her hair. Leaving the store, she eyed a phone booth near the door. Picking up the directory, Jennie looked up Chavez. She'd forgotten to ask Tess and Agent Tucker about Crystal Chavez. And they hadn't mentioned her. Jennie was certain the nurse held the key to Scott's disappearance. Mrs. Casey had refused to give her Crystal's phone number, but US West was much kinder. By now she imagined the FBI agents would have talked with her and anyone else who'd had any connection with Scott last night. Still, it wouldn't hurt to find out where she lived and maybe drive by. Jennie wrote the address and phone number down, then checked out the map in the directory and climbed back into the car.

Crystal's house was a small one-story on the left side of the street. Either she'd parked her car in the garage or she'd gone somewhere. Jennie parked on the opposite side of the street about half a block away. She sat there for five minutes looking at the white house with blue trim. The curtains were drawn and she could see no signs of life. *You should leave,* she told herself. If Crystal was in on the abduction and had drugged her, being anywhere near this place could be dangerous. Scott could be hidden inside, guarded by armed terrorists. The FBI agents Tucker had mentioned could be imprisoned in there, too, and the missing deputy.

On the other hand, maybe the FBI agents were watching the place. Jennie looked up and down the street but saw no indication of a surveillance crew, FBI or otherwise.

Five more minutes and Jennie couldn't stand it. She had to know if Crystal was home. She'd march up to the front door, and if Crystal answered, she'd ask straight out what had happened to Scott.

Jennie drew in a deep breath and stepped out of her car. Locking it, she pocketed the keys and concentrated on putting one foot in front of the other. Every step brought her closer to the door and whatever lay behind it. Jennie cleared her head of the thoughts of terrorists hiding inside and of Crystal being a murderer and greeting her at the door with an automatic rifle.

She's a nurse, Jennie reminded herself. *Someone who's committed to saving lives.* She imagined the kind, caring Crystal inviting her in and telling her . . . what, that she'd lost Scott?

The white door with a black security screen loomed in front

of her. *It's not too late to back out.* Almost on its own volition, Jennie's hand reached out. Her forefinger pressed the doorbell. She held her breath. Listening so intently for sounds from within, Jennie almost missed the car that pulled up in front of the house. Someone was coming up the walk. She swallowed hard. Had Crystal come home? Was it an FBI agent? Or someone from ARM? Jennie slowly turned around to face the mysterious visitor.

"Why, Jennie. What are you doing here?" Christine Sutherland stepped onto the porch.

"I . . . I met Crystal last night while she was taking care of Scott and—"

"Scott? You mean the Chambers boy. He's in the hospital?" The concern on Christine's face brought Jennie's fears into submission.

"He was hurt in a hit-and-run accident—well, I don't believe it was an accident. I think someone was trying to kill him."

"I—I don't know what to say. Who'd want to do something like that?"

"That's what I'm trying to find out."

"How is he?"

Jennie frowned and decided to level with Christine. "He's gone. Someone drugged me and abducted him from the hospital last night."

"Are you serious?" She stared openmouthed at Jennie.

"He's gone, all right, and the hospital has no record of his having been there. I think it might have been someone from ARM, and I think Crystal might have some information, but she doesn't seem to be home."

"No, she isn't. She's gone camping for a few days. She called this morning and asked me to come over and feed her cat."

"So you know Crystal fairly well?"

"My yes. She and Aleshia went all through school together. They're the best of friends."

"Is Crystal a member of ARM too?"

"Not that I know of. Crystal cares about animals, of course, but . . . I hope you're not insinuating that Crystal had something to do with your friend's disappearance."

"I don't know what to think. I came by here hoping she'd be able to tell me something about it. She was on duty last night, and

I can't imagine her not knowing if one of her patients disappears."

"That is strange, but I'm afraid you'll have to wait until she gets back." Christine inserted a key into the lock and pulled open the screen door. Using another key, she opened the white door.

"When will that be?" Jennie followed her inside.

"Tuesday, I think." Christine headed for the kitchen. "Here, kitty. Come on, baby. Time to eat."

"Meow." A huge white cat stretched, then gathered itself together, jumping off the window ledge and prancing into the kitchen, its tail high and twitching.

"Do you know where she is?" Jennie's gaze scanned the simple but nicely decorated home. Neat. Nothing out of place except books that spilled out of an overflowing bookcase. Family pictures hung on one wall. A Bible sat on an end table along with a devotional book called *365 Saints*. A rosary lay beside it.

"I'm afraid not. Crystal is hiking and could be anywhere."

Jennie moved over to the phone near the sofa and glanced down at the pad. There was no writing on it, only an indentation from a previous note. She tore off the top sheet and tucked it into her back pocket, then moved to the kitchen. "Beautiful cat."

"Yes, she is." Christine rinsed the cat's dish in the sink and filled one side with water and the other with food. The cat wrapped itself around her legs. "Here you go," she cooed as she rubbed the cat behind the ears.

"I'm worried about Crystal." Jennie leaned against the doorjamb and watched the cat eat. "If she wasn't involved in Scott's disappearance, whoever took him might have her too."

Christine rubbed her wrinkled forehead. "Does Tess know about this?"

"Yes. She and an agent are looking into it. They're on their way out to your place to ask you and Aleshia some questions."

"They think we had something to do with Scott's disappearance?"

"They think your husband might have."

"Bob? But he's missing too."

"Maybe—" Jennie stopped herself. Better not to mention their suspicions about her husband's involvement in ARM. It occurred to her that if Bob Sutherland was Sonja, Christine would undoubtedly know something about it. She'd already said too much. "I don't know what's going on. It's way too confusing."

"Hmm. You're right about that. I'd better get back. I probably shouldn't have left, but—it's so hard sitting around the house. I went out with the S and R team this morning for a while. I just wish I knew what happened to him. And now your friend. It's frightening."

"You can say that again." Jennie followed her out the door and down the walk.

"I hope they find your friend, Jennie." Christine got into her car and glanced around. "Do you need a ride?"

"No, I parked down the street." At Christine's questioning look, Jennie added, "I like to walk."

"I'll wait until you're safely on your way. The last thing we need is for something to happen to you." Christine waited until Jennie got in her car and pulled away before leaving, then followed Jennie as far as the Sutherlands' driveway.

The sheriff and Agent Tucker were still waiting. Jennie wished she could be a fly on the wall, but they'd given her explicit orders to stay away. There wasn't much to do now except shower, change clothes, and maybe get some sleep. All of which sounded heavenly.

Tom and Mary's car was gone, but the door had been left unlocked. Jennie glanced at the table, wondering if they'd left a note, but saw none. Taking the steps two at a time, Jennie checked on the wounded mink, then headed for the bathroom and a much-needed shower.

After a two-hour nap, the telephone jangled, and Jennie hurried into Tom and Mary's bedroom/office suite to get it.

"Jennie," Lisa said. "I was about to give up on you."

"I was sleeping." She sank into the leather office chair.

"Oh, I'm sorry. I just wanted to let you know where we were— forgot to leave a note."

"So where are you?"

"At the Sutherlands'. Mom wanted to check on Christine. The sheriff and an agent came to question her and Aleshia."

"Did they find Mr. Sutherland or Scott?"

"Not yet. This is all so weird."

"I'm surprised you and Megan are still there."

"You should be here too, Jen. This is a real mystery."

"Well, take notes for me. I want to know everything they said." Glancing down at her bare feet, she added, "I'll be there in about ten minutes."

Setting the phone back into the cradle, Jennie glanced at a fat file sitting on the bedside stand. It was labeled ARM. She opened the folder. It held alarming materials from an Internet address. One was entitled "Electronically Timed Incendiary Devices" with directions for making and concealing them. Placed in stores where furs are sold, they cause a fire large enough to turn on the store's sprinkler system, which damages or destroys the merchandise and costs the store thousands. At the end the article included this tip: *Arson is a felony, so wear gloves. Be careful not to leave evidence.*

Jennie quickly scanned some disturbing articles: "Maximum Destruction NOT Minimum Damage," "Smashing the Furriers," and another on the use of fire. There was one long article from an anonymous person who was involved with ARM. Overall the file contained lists of fur farms and detailed instructions on how to destroy or debilitate them.

She felt sick. Why would John and Mary have information like this in their home? Was it a means of knowing the enemy, or were they underground members of ARM?

Jennie returned the papers to the manila file and left it where she'd found it and returned to Megan's bedroom. If she'd had any doubt about the integrity of animal rights activists, it was gone now. These people were criminals, pure and simple.

She stuffed her feet into socks and her Reeboks, slipped on a sweat shirt, and brushed her hair into a ponytail. Setting her brush on the dresser, she noticed the blank notepaper she'd pulled off the pad at Crystal's place. Finding a pencil, she lightly shaded the paper until the writing appeared in white. Jennie wrinkled her nose in disappointment. It was nothing but a grocery list.

Jennie tossed the paper in the trash and headed downstairs. She didn't bother with a jacket, since the day had turned sunny and warm.

Jennie debated taking her car but decided to walk over. She

needed the exercise, and the fresh air felt good. The file she'd seen at Tom and Mary's haunted her. How could people who seemingly cared so much about animals talk about torching department stores and restaurants? They were primarily vegetarians with their own set of rules and beliefs. In thinking about it, she realized that Tom and Mary couldn't be involved with ARM. They were definitely meat eaters.

When she approached the Sutherland house, Megan and Lisa came out to meet her. "What took you so long?" Lisa hooked her arm around Jennie's.

"I, um—" Jennie looked at Megan. "I answered the phone in your parents' room and—"

"Is something wrong?"

"Not exactly, I'm just curious. I was hanging up the phone when I spotted a file labeled ARM on the desk."

"So?"

"So I got a little nervous about it. Why would your folks keep stuff like that?"

"Oh. I guess it would be kind of creepy coming across their articles. Mom and Dad get all kinds of stuff about ARM. The Fur Commission wants everyone to know what kinds of information ARM is putting out. We need to know what we're up against."

"I can see why." Relieved, Jennie changed the subject. "What's going on over here? I see that Tess and Agent Tucker are gone."

"They just left. They found the deputy who was supposed to be taking care of Scott."

"Did they say what had happened to him?"

Megan sneered. "The owner of our town's only tavern found him in the alley propped up beside the dumpster."

"Had he been drinking?" Jennie asked.

"I guess. Tess seemed pretty steamed about it."

"I can see why." Jennie sighed. "I wonder . . ."

"What?"

"Well, I think someone slipped something in my tea to knock me out while they took Scott away. The nurse who took care of him is missing. Someone erased all of Scott's records. And now they find the guard in an alley. I'll bet he hadn't been drinking. Maybe they drugged him too. I should go talk to Tess."

"We'll go with you," Lisa and Megan said together.

"Hey, Megan!" The shout came from the machine shop. Jim stood in the opening. "Tell your dad to get down here on the double. And call the sheriff!"

"What's going on?"

"You don't want to know. Just get them. Now!"

Megan pinched her lips together and tromped up the stairs. "He can be so rude."

Jennie glanced at Jim, then back at Megan. "What's he doing over here?"

"Christine called him this morning to see if he could help feed the mink. With Bob missing, they were falling behind schedule. Dad!" Megan opened the door and leaned inside. "Jim says to get down there right away."

"What's going on?" Tom set his coffee cup on the counter and headed out the door.

"I don't know, but he sounds upset. I'm supposed to call the sheriff."

Tom and Mary exchanged glances. He passed Jennie in the doorway looking worried. Jennie felt torn. Should she stay in the house or follow Tom to the shed? Her curiosity won and Jennie yelled, "I'm going with him."

She jogged after Tom, but by the time she'd reached the shed, she saw no sign of either man.

"Mr. Bergstom? What's going on?"

"Stay out, Jennie." Tom came around the corner, leaned over, and vomited on the floor. He waved her away when she took a step toward him.

"Get back to the house," he ordered, "and get the sheriff out here." He rose and came toward her. "Tell her—" He held his stomach and looked like he was going to be sick again. "Tell her we found Bob."

"Is he. . . ?"

"He's dead, Jennie. Now go."

15

The horror of Tom's words seeped into her soul as she ran back to the house. Megan and Lisa had come out. She warned them not to go down to the shop. "Jim found Mr. Sutherland. He's dead."

"Do you know how it happened?" Lisa asked.

She shook her head. "We'll find out soon enough. Did you get ahold of the sheriff?"

"Her cell phone was busy," Megan responded, "so I left a message with the dispatcher to call."

"Not good enough." Jennie jogged the short distance to the house. "Where's the phone?" Mary and Christine both pointed to the kitchen counter.

"What is it, Jennie?" Mary asked. "What's going on?"

Jennie crossed the room, picked up the receiver, and punched in 9–1–1. She turned around and leaned on the counter, looking at Mary, then Christine, as she spoke.

"Yes," she said when the emergency operator responded. "This is Jennie McGrady. We need the sheriff at the Sutherland farm right away. Mr. Sutherland . . ." She gulped at the stricken look on Christine's face. "No, it's not an injury. Mr. Sutherland is dead."

"I'm sorry," Jennie said as she replaced the receiver. "I guess I shouldn't have blurted it out like that."

Christine stared into her coffee. "I think deep down I must have known all along." She pushed back her chair. Her napkin fell to the floor. "Poor Jim. If I'd known, I would never have asked him to help out today. I should go talk to him."

"Better that Jim found him than you." Mary patted Christine's hand.

"I need to call Aleshia." Christine stood.

"Would you like me to do that?" Mary offered.

"Thanks, but no. I'll do it." She left the room and made her way upstairs, apparently needing the privacy of her bedroom.

Mary went to the oven, slipped on an oven mitt, and took out a pan of cookies. They smelled warm and homey and normal. "She was running low," Mary explained. "With so many people coming and going she was worried she'd run out."

Looking over at Jennie and Lisa, she said, "I'm afraid this hasn't been a very good time for you girls."

"It's okay," Lisa said. "You couldn't have known. . . ."

Jennie didn't respond. It was one of those odd statements people said when they were in shock. "Christine said she was going to call Aleshia. Isn't she here?"

"No."

"Where did she go?"

"I'm not sure. Back to Portland I suppose."

"Listen. Sirens," Megan said.

Jennie set her questions about Aleshia aside, then followed Megan and Lisa out to the porch and down the stairs. Tess cut the sirens as she approached the house and got out of her car. "Where are they?"

"In the machine shop," Jennie said.

Tom stepped out of the shop and waved the sheriff over. "We haven't touched anything except for when Jim opened the box. Looks like someone gassed him."

Jennie's insides crumbled. Gassed. As in carbon monoxide—the deadly gas the farmers used to kill the mink. She covered her mouth thinking she might be sick.

"Did you hear that?" Lisa grabbed Jennie's arm.

"I heard."

"I can't stand it," Megan whimpered. "Who could have done something so awful?"

"I'm wondering the same thing." Jennie did a quick calculation. "Mr. Sutherland disappeared yesterday shortly after Scott left."

"Are you thinking he did it?"

"No. But he might know who did. Suppose he witnessed it or figured it out. The murderer might have gone after Scott and run him down." She frowned. "But if that was the case, why didn't he say something at the hospital?"

"I don't know." Tears filled Megan's eyes.

Lisa bit her lip. "I sure hope he's okay, Jennie."

"I can't stand to talk about it anymore." Megan sniffled. "I need a Kleenex."

"I have some." Jennie pulled a box of tissues out of the Mustang and handed it to her.

Lisa sighed. "M-maybe we could do something to get our minds off all this. It's warm enough to swim."

"I'd like that. Maybe the guys would like to come too." Megan wiped her eyes and blew her nose.

"You two go ahead. I want to stick around for a little while."

"I'm not sure that's a good idea, Jennie," Lisa said. "Mr. Sutherland is dead. Scott is missing. I'm afraid that if you get too involved, something might happen to you too. You know what happened last time."

Jennie rolled her eyes. "Don't remind me. Anyway, that was different. I was in the hospital parking lot alone."

"You were trying to figure out who burned down our school."

"I'm not getting involved in this one. Not really. I'm just curious, that's all. And I'm worried about Scott."

"We are too," Lisa insisted. "Maybe we should stay here too."

"Don't be silly. Nothing's going to happen to me here. The place will be swarming with cops in a minute."

Jennie had no sooner uttered the words when three more emergency vehicles pulled into the driveway—Agent Tucker and the two deputies who'd scoured the lake for Sutherland. Two minutes later a deputy medical examiner showed up with an ambulance on his tail. The investigation had begun in earnest.

Jennie did a lot of pacing over the next hour. Lisa and Megan had finally gone back to Megan's place to change into swimsuits and call Algie and Kyle. Jennie promised to meet them at the lake later. She probably should have gone with them, but she couldn't bear to leave until she'd learned the facts.

Tess, Agent Tucker, and the medical examiner would be investigating the body and the crime scene, comparing notes, and drawing conclusions from the evidence. That had to be the hardest part of police work. Gathering evidence at the scene of a murder. This was what her father did as a homicide detective. Somehow she'd always glamorized the job. Now she realized how awful it could be having to deal with murder on a daily basis. No wonder he looked so stressed when he came home from work. Jennie had no desire to see them in action but desperately wanted to hear the details about how Bob Sutherland had been killed.

Tess came out of the shed, raking a hand through her hair. "You still here, Jennie?"

"I couldn't go without knowing what happened to him. With Scott missing . . ." Jennie couldn't finish.

"We'll find him. We're talking to the hospital staff now."

"I heard you found your volunteer deputy."

"Right. He'd been drinking and apparently stumbled into an alley. We still haven't found the nurse."

"Crystal is camping—until Tuesday. At least that's what Christine says." Jennie went on to tell her about the encounter they'd had at Crystal's house.

Tess heaved an exasperated sigh. "That was a stupid thing to do. What if it hadn't been Christine? Jennie, that nurse may have been an accomplice."

"I know. I just wanted to find him. I thought if I could just talk to Crystal—"

"We're dealing with ruthless criminals here. And unless you want to end up like Mr. Sutherland, you'll keep your nose out of it. If you don't, I'll call your parents to come get you. The last thing I need around here is a nosy kid who fancies herself the next Nancy Drew."

"You don't need to do that."

"Look, I know how you must feel. You care very much for Scott, and I can see why. He's a nice kid, but he got in over his head. The FBI shouldn't have used him like they did. Tucker admitted that. You can bet they're busting their britches to find him."

Jennie stared down at her shoes. "I'm sorry. You're right. I shouldn't have gone to Crystal's house."

Tess backed down and nodded in the direction of the shed. "I'm sorry too—didn't mean to bite your head off. Murder is a nasty business. I meant what I said though."

"I don't plan on doing any more investigating on my own, but I'd still like to know what happened to Mr. Sutherland."

Tess shook her head. "You'll read about it in the paper tomorrow anyway, so I suppose it wouldn't hurt. You can come with us to talk to Christine."

"Us?"

"Tucker will be along in a minute."

One by one the two deputies, Jim Owens, Tom, and the medical examiner filed out of the building. The two paramedics who'd arrived with the ambulance came next, maneuvering a stretcher carrying the large, covered form of Bob Sutherland between them.

"The ME promised a preliminary report this afternoon." Tucker's troubled gaze stayed on the body until the ambulance doors closed. "Never gets any easier, does it?"

"I'm told that's a good thing."

"So I hear. You ready to question the widow?"

"Ready as I'll ever be. You want to talk to her or should I?"

"You do it. When we get to the pelt, I'll take over."

Pelt? What pelt? Jennie didn't dare ask. Instead, she tagged along behind, trying to look invisible. The less conspicuous she remained, the better her chances of picking up information.

Once inside, they sat around the table. Jennie stood near the door where they couldn't see her. Out of sight, out of mind.

Tess and Agent Tucker gratefully accepted the coffee Mary offered. After pouring herself a cup, she set the tray of freshly baked cookies on the table, then sat down next to Christine. Tess took several sips before she spoke. "The medical examiner figures your husband died about twenty-four hours ago."

"About the time he went missing." Christine closed her eyes. "I shouldn't have gone into town. Maybe if I'd been here—"

"Don't blame yourself," Mary said.

"How—how did it happen?" Christine straightened as if bracing herself.

"We'll have more details after the autopsy, but he was apparently struck on the head with a blunt instrument—probably his hammer. He may have been removing a pelt at the time."

Christine covered her face with her hands. "Do you know who did it?"

"We have some ideas." Tess reached for a cookie and broke it in half. "The hammer isn't what killed him. The killer put him in the gas chamber and pumped it full of carbon monoxide."

"Oh no." Christine looked ready to break.

"It was ARM, wasn't it?" Mary asked. "They killed him in the same way he killed the animals."

"It was them, all right," Jim piped up. "I've never known them to come back and kill the owner, but maybe they're getting more aggressive."

"You may be right," Tess said. "There's something else. Whoever killed him left a signature—used a marker to write an X on his back."

A sound like that of a wounded animal escaped Christine's throat. "I don't think I want to hear any more."

"Look, why don't you let her be? She's been through enough." Jim stood up and went around to stand behind his future mother-in-law, his large hands cupping her thin shoulders.

"I know this is hard." Tess softened. "We can finish up later if you need to stop."

Christine shook her head. "It won't be any easier then."

"Well, we know one thing. The blood we found all over the counters wasn't Bob's," Tess said.

"Blood?" Christine looked up at Tess.

"On the counter in the shop. Jim found it, but by the time I got there to check it out, someone had cleaned it up."

Christine rubbed her forehead. "I'm afraid that was me." She glanced guiltily at Mary, then back at Tess. "I went upstairs and took a sleeping pill, but I still couldn't sleep. I thought maybe if I looked in the shed again . . . When I went out and saw the mess, all I could think of was how upset Bob would be when he got back. I suppose that sounds rather insane. It didn't occur to me that I might be disturbing a crime scene. I'm sorry."

"Oh, Christine," Mary sighed. "It's not insane. You were beside yourself. I understand perfectly."

Tucker rubbed a hand across his jaw. "I'm glad someone does. Why did you sneak out? Mary thought you were asleep."

"I didn't sneak out. I just went out the back way—it's where I keep my boots. By the time I finished cleaning I felt exhausted—came back in and fell asleep. Mary was busy in the kitchen and I didn't feel like talking."

Tucker nodded. "No real harm done, Mrs. Sutherland. Can you think of anyone who might want to kill your husband?"

"You mean, did he have enemies? I'm afraid so. Would any of them kill him? I have no idea."

"Straight Edgers." Mary shifted her gaze to Tess.

"What?" Tess set her cup down and scribbled something on her note pad.

"I read about them in the paper a few months ago." Mary took a sip of coffee. "They're young people who are anti-drugs, smoking, and casual sex. For the most part they're vegetarians and came out of the punk rock scene of the '80s. The subculture is fairly large, but only a few of them have turned violent."

"Those few have caused a lot of damage," Tucker said. "A number of them have linked up with ARM and have been torching fast-food restaurants, fur-trapping outfits, and fur farms. They hate anyone who eats meat."

"Yes, I remember." Christine dabbed at her eyes with a tissue. "The fur commission sent a fax."

"Do you have a copy?" Mary asked.

"I'm sure I do. I'll get my files."

Tess set her pen down and reached for her cup. "Don't bother. Now that you mention it, I do remember seeing some memos come in from the FBI about them. They're also called Hate Edgers. Scary group. We haven't been bothered by them before now."

"We've run into a few in Portland." Tucker rubbed his chin. "They say no to drugs and yes to fire bombs."

"Christine," Tess went on, "tell me again about yesterday. Everything that led up to your husband's disappearance."

"I told you everything already."

"I know, but I'd like Agent Tucker to hear it as well."

Christine seemed to gather herself. "Bob didn't sleep at all after the raid. I've never seen him so angry. Said he knew the Chambers kid was in on it and insisted he was going to beat the information out of him. I tried to talk some sense into him, and when he wouldn't listen I went with him. He had his gun, but I took that when we got to the Bergstroms' place and wouldn't give it back. I told him he was going to have to kill me first.

"Bob swore at me but didn't press it. He went into the bunkhouse, found Scott packing his things, and started beating on him. Scott ran out of the house, and Bob tore after him. That's when Tom and Jennie showed up. With Tom's help we were able to get Bob calmed down. I thought it was over. His back was hurting and he'd gone upstairs to lie down. I called Aleshia and asked her to meet me for lunch. I left around ten-thirty. I was so angry at Bob I . . ."

Christine's face clouded over and she reached for another tissue. "I'm sorry. I didn't even kiss him good-bye when I left. The next thing I knew Bob was gone. I guess Stan had come by to tell him he had to go to Portland—a family emergency. Stan got worried when he couldn't find him and called around. You know the rest."

"Where is Stan now?" Jennie asked.

"I'll ask the questions, Jennie." Tess twisted around and shot her a keep-out-of-this look.

"Sorry, I thought maybe the call was bogus to get Mr. Sutherland out of the way. I still don't think Scott did it."

"The call was legitimate," Christine offered. "His mother had fallen and broken her hip. He's still there. Will be for another week or so. He called me yesterday."

"Now that we've satisfied Jennie's curiosity, I'd like to get back to your meeting with Aleshia. You left here at ten-thirty and met Aleshia in town when?"

"At noon. I went shopping first."

"Where was Aleshia during that time?" Tess asked.

Had Aleshia come out to the farm, killed her father, then gone into town to meet Christine? There would have been time.

"Oh no, Sheriff." Christine must have caught on as well.

"You're not thinking Aleshia could have . . . No! She and her father didn't get along, but Aleshia isn't a killer. Besides, didn't you say Jim found him in the . . . box?"

"That's right," Agent Tucker answered.

"Aleshia couldn't have lifted him into it."

"True. But it doesn't take that much strength to operate a lift truck." He cleared his throat.

Mary gasped. "Oh, how awful."

"My guess," Tucker went on, "is that the killer sneaked up on him from behind, took the hammer from the tool belt while he was working on a pelt, and hit him in the back of the head, then gassed him to finish the job. Your daughter is a member of ARM."

"I'm sorry, Christine," Tess said. "I know this is hard, but she has motive, and statistics show that most murders are committed by family members or people who know the victim."

"I don't care about your statistics, Tess Parker. I know my daughter. Nothing would provoke her to . . . to commit murder."

"I'm not so sure about that." Agent Tucker got to his feet. "Would you come with me to the shop, please?"

"What . . . Why?" She rose from her chair and followed the FBI agent outside and into the sunlight.

"There's something in the shed I'd like you to see."

Jennie trailed along behind, hoping it wasn't the body, but then realized it couldn't be because an ambulance had already come and removed it.

The five of them walked without speaking. Jennie hesitated before going in. Jennie held her breath as Agent Tucker opened the heavy door to the freezer. He came out a moment later carrying a plastic bag with an animal carcass inside. "We think this is what Mr. Sutherland was skinning when he died."

Mary covered her mouth and closed her eyes.

Christine stared at the half-skinned animal, and a look of horror filled her eyes.

Jennie looked away from the dead animal. She couldn't be sure, but it looked like the fox she'd picked up in the yard the night of the release.

"It's Sasha, Aleshia's pet fox." Jim stepped in front of Christine, shielding her. "Sutherland didn't care who he hurt. He did it to spite her. I . . . I killed him."

16

"No, Jim." Christine tried to pull him back. "Don't say any more. We'll get a lawyer."

Jim Owens took in several ragged breaths. "It's no use, Christine. They'd find out sooner or later. I might as well come clean." He turned back to Tucker. "Have someone take Christine back to the house. I'll tell you everything."

"You don't need to do this." Christine cast pleading eyes in his direction.

"Yes, I do."

Silent words flew between them. Jennie wished she could intercept, but all she could do was venture a guess. Jim's admission of guilt came at the moment he saw the carcass of Aleshia's pet fox. The anguish etched across his face, and his comment to Christine that he had to confess led Jennie to question the validity of his statement. Jennie had read mysteries where a family member confessed to a crime he didn't commit—willing to face prison and death to save a loved one. Was Jim that kind of person?

Christine backed down and let Mary lead her away. Did she think her daughter was guilty as well?

Jim waited until they'd gone, then gave his confession. "I came over to talk to Bob yesterday morning about some money he owed me. When I saw what he was doing, I confronted him. I couldn't believe he'd do something so hateful. He laughed at me. 'Serves her right. I never thought she'd set me up,' he said. I told him he was wrong and that Aleshia didn't have anything to do with the releases in this area. He wouldn't listen. I'd had it with him. Ale-

119

shia's a good person. She's got her priorities a little messed up, but she'd never intentionally hurt anyone."

"For pete's sake, Jim, don't do this to yourself." Tom turned to the officers. "He was working for me yesterday. He couldn't have killed Bob."

"Stay out of this, okay? I was gone for over half an hour, remember?" Jim's hands shook as he stretched them out to Agent Tucker. "Go ahead and arrest me. I killed him. I saw what he was doing and lost it. The hammer was hanging on the tool belt where he always kept it. I grabbed it and hit him. It didn't kill him, so I put him in the box and turned on the gas. I wanted to get rid of the evidence and throw everyone off track, so I drove his tractor into the lake and tossed in his gloves and hammer. I came back to the shop, wrapped up Sasha, and stuck the pelt in the freezer so Aleshia wouldn't see it. Thought I'd bury it later. He had no business hurting her like that. Aleshia and Christine will both be better off without him. I'm glad I killed him."

Tess's eyes narrowed. Tucker gave her a quick nod. They weren't falling for his line either. It surprised Jennie when Tess pulled out a pair of cuffs, turned him around, and placed his hands behind him. "Jim Owens, I'm placing you under arrest for the murder of Bob Sutherland. You have the right to remain silent. . . ." She finished Mirandizing him and led him to the car and settled him into the backseat.

She came back to the door of the shop, where Jennie, Tom, and Agent Tucker were waiting. "Well, what do you think?"

"He's lying," Tom said. "Trying to protect Aleshia, I suspect. He took off for about a half hour yesterday morning like he said, but there's no way anyone could kill a man like that and go back to work like nothing happened."

"Don't be too sure about that." Agent Tucker nodded toward Owens. "He's lying, all right, but we need to play along with him for now. Having him in custody might work to our advantage. If Aleshia did kill her father, I suspect she'll come clean rather than let her fiancé go to prison."

"How can you be sure he's lying?" Jennie asked. "I mean—I thought so too, but . . ."

"His confession has a gaping hole in it." Tucker settled a hand on her shoulder. "He said he put the fox in the freezer. He couldn't have. I found it in the trash behind the building and set it in the refrigeration unit myself."

"Are you going to arrest Aleshia?" Jennie asked.

"Not yet. We'll bring her in for questioning." Tess hitched up her gun belt. "We'll see how it goes from there."

"Um—what if she did it and doesn't confess?" Jennie asked. "She might realize that there isn't sufficient evidence to convict him. You know Jim didn't do it, but what if he keeps insisting? Do you go to trial?"

"Hopefully it won't get that far." Tucker reminded her not to talk about the case to anyone.

"I won't," Jennie assured him. As they walked she asked about Scott again.

"I wish I had good news for you. Unfortunately, we still can't find his hospital records. We know he was there, of course, but we still haven't been able to locate the nurse. Her family claims they don't know where she is. The guard couldn't tell us anything. We've questioned everyone who was on the floor that night. They only had a couple of nurses working that section."

"Scary to think someone could be abducted from a hospital."

"Well, that's another thing. According to the ER doctor, it's possible Scott walked out on his own. All he needed was someone to bring him a pair of crutches." Tucker pulled his keys out of his pocket.

"I don't believe that. He was in so much pain, along with the concussion."

"That brings up another possibility. The head injury could have caused some confusion."

"You're not giving up, are you?" Jenny tucked her hair behind her ear.

"No. One way or another, we'll find him." He reached for the door handle, then turned back to her. "There's one more thing you should be aware of, Jennie. Scott was supposed to be working for us. But there's also the possibility he used us to gain information for ARM."

Jennie could hardly believe what she was hearing. "Like a double agent?"

"It wouldn't be the first time."

"Not Scott. What about the hit-and-run? Somebody tried to kill him."

"We don't know that for sure. It may have been unrelated. Scott told Tess he didn't have any idea who might have hit him. Couldn't give us any of the details—or wouldn't."

Jennie folded her arms and backed away when he shifted into reverse. Tess had already started down the drive.

Tom gave Jennie a fatherly hug. "Scott's lucky to have a friend like you, Jennie. I hope he's deserving of it."

Jennie hoped so, too, but didn't say so.

"Let's see how Mary and Christine are doing."

They were nearly to the porch when Mary came out and shut the door behind her. "Are you two ready to go home?"

"You're not staying with her?" Tom asked.

"Christine called a lawyer. She's meeting him at the sheriff's office in an hour. She wants to take a shower before she goes. No point in my being here. She seems to be handling things all right. I'm sure it helps having something to do. She's worried sick about Aleshia—hasn't been able to reach her."

"Maybe her lawyer can straighten this out. Jim is a fool for making a confession like that."

"I'm sure he felt it was the noble thing to do."

"Noble, my foot." Tom opened the door to his pickup. "His jumping in with a confession has done nothing more than cast more suspicion on Aleshia."

"I'm sure it will all be cleared up soon, and the authorities will realize that neither Aleshia nor Jim had anything to do with it. This is obviously the act of terrorists."

Tom slid in and closed the door.

"Would you like a ride back to the house, Jennie?" Mary offered before getting in.

"No, thanks. I'll walk. Lisa and Megan might still be down by the lake."

"See you later, then." They backed around and waved as they passed her. Jennie felt a mingling of relief and uneasiness as they drove away. A haunting silence surrounded her. Only one vehicle remained in the yard now—Christine's deep purple Bonneville.

Hairs on the back of her neck stood on end. Something didn't seem right, but Jennie couldn't think what it might be.

"Jennie?" Christine called down to her from an upstairs window. "Is everything all right? I thought everyone had gone."

"I'm just leaving." Jennie glanced over at the car again. It stood there alone. Like Mrs. Sutherland. *Of course, that's it.* "Um, Mrs. Sutherland, I just noticed your husband's truck is gone. It was here yesterday and—"

Christine stared blankly at the space where the truck should have been. "You're right. I can't believe I didn't notice it before. Someone must have stolen it." She ran a hand through her hair. "That's all I need right now."

"Would you like me to call the sheriff?"

"No, I'll tell her when I go into the office. Thanks for all your help, Jennie." She ducked back inside, closed the window, and lowered the blinds.

"You're welcome." Jennie tucked her fingers into the pockets of her jeans and started down the road to the lake. While she walked, her mind replayed the disjointed events in what now had become a murder case. The raid on Sutherlands' place. Bob's disappearance the next day, which they now knew to be his death. The bizarre circumstances of the death itself. Had the killer set it up to make it look like a gang killing? Then the hit-and-run, which may or may not have been an attempt on Scott's life. Scott's disappearance, or whatever it was, and now the missing truck. She wouldn't be at all surprised to learn that whoever had run down Scott had stolen the truck and that the police would eventually find it abandoned somewhere. Thoughts of Scott set her heart to aching again. She didn't know how long she could stand waiting while the FBI searched for him. *I just wish there was something I could do.*

The afternoon sun was beating down on the water, and swimming seemed the perfect way to work out the tension that had settled into her shoulders. Jennie spotted the foursome sitting on the dock and waved, glad they'd waited for her. She jogged the rest of the way.

Jennie yelled greetings to the swimmers, saying she'd get changed and join them. Ten minutes later, she slipped off her shoes, dropped her cover-up and towel, and dove into the lake. It felt deliciously cold against her too-warm skin. She swam out to the middle and back several times. The exercise, as it always did, cleared her head and gave her a new perspective. She needed to trust the authorities to find Scott and deal with the murder investigation. It would be hard not to get involved, but what else could she do?

She reached for the dock and pulled herself up. Algie and Kyle had their shirts on and were tying their shoes. "You two leaving already?" She reached for her towel and wrapped it around herself.

Algie nodded. "We both have chores to do. We'll be over to pick you up later, though."

Megan knelt down behind him and wrapped her arms around his neck. "You guys are really sweet to do this."

Kyle sighed. "Yeah, that's us."

Jennie looked from one to the other. "What are you planning to do?"

Lisa beamed. "We're going to help you find out what happened to Scott."

Jennie squeezed the water out of her ponytail. "Look, guys, I'm not sure that's such a good idea. I got strict orders from Sheriff Parker and Agent Tucker to sit tight."

"Oh, we won't be doing anything dangerous," Lisa assured her. "Algie and Kyle have a friend whose last name happens to be Chavez and who happens to know where we can find Crystal."

"So," Megan said, "he's promised to take us to her."

"Where is she?" Jennie's breath caught. This was the best news she'd had all day.

"He won't say." Algie scrambled to his feet. "He's afraid to tell anyone because he knows the cops are looking for her."

"We told him about the deal with Scott and how he was your boyfriend and everything," Kyle said. "Sal will take us there, but we have to promise not to let the cops know."

Jennie pulled on her cover-up. "We should tell Agent Tucker."

"No, Jennie." Kyle stood up and took hold of her shoulders.

"We promised. Besides, the cops already talked to him."

"I don't know. It could be dangerous."

"Sal is a good friend." Kyle's concerned gaze caught hers. "He wouldn't be taking us there if he thought there'd be trouble."

Jennie was weakening. She did want to talk to Crystal. And being with four other people should be safe enough. "Okay, let's do it. What will you tell your parents, Megan?"

"The truth—that we're going for a drive."

At six that evening, Algie, Kyle, and Sal drove into the Bergstroms' driveway. Megan and Lisa were already downstairs. Jennie looked out the window, still struggling with the idea of not telling Agent Tucker. What if something happened? Still, if going with Sal was the only way to talk to Crystal, she couldn't pass up the opportunity. In a last-minute decision, Jennie jotted a quick note:

Dear Tom and Mary,
    We've gone with Sal Chavez, Crystal's brother. He knows where Crystal is but says he won't talk to the police. If anything happens and we don't come back, see that Agent Tucker gets this.

She signed it and set it on the bedside stand against the lamp.

"Jennie!" Lisa called. "They're here."

"Coming." Jennie took a deep breath to steady herself. "You're doing the right thing," she whispered to the voice inside her that kept saying, *No.*

17

"I'm beginning to wish we hadn't come." Lisa cringed with every bump the four-wheel-drive truck maneuvered around. "I was expecting a state park and pavement."

"It's a little late for second thoughts." Jennie's hopes of being able to tell the FBI where to find Crystal Chavez when they returned to civilization were dashed ten minutes after they exited the main road. They'd been driving for over an hour, and all she knew was they were in the mountains somewhere between Salem and Sisters, traveling on a narrow, rutted logging road in the middle of nowhere. She'd seen no road signs, but then, this wasn't exactly a freeway. The curved, tree-lined road seemed to be taking them in circles.

"I hope we're getting close." Jennie leaned forward, placing her arms on the front seat behind Kyle's head. "I swear this backseat was designed for pygmies."

"It's not much farther." Sal turned around and flashed her a grin. The glistening white teeth were about all she could see of him in the dark cab. Outside was even darker. He turned back around to look at the mileage meter. "Another mile or so."

Jennie sighed and sank back. "You sure she's up here?"

"I'm sure."

Some of Jennie's earlier fears had subsided after talking with Sal. He had an easy smile and gentle nature—at least that had been her impression. Unlike his sister, he still had a Spanish accent and every once in a while slipped into his native tongue. He seemed confident and outgoing. He was about five six with an athletic build, wavy brown hair, a wide face, and big, trusting brown eyes—like Crystal's. She patted the small tape recorder that lay in one of the pockets of the down parka Megan had loaned her.

She'd already recorded her conversation with Sal. He'd disclosed nothing about his sister's whereabouts, only indicated that they would need warm clothing and survival gear in case they had car trouble.

The deep woods lay dark and threatening out the window of Algie's truck. Jennie's anxiety returned full force. They'd been stupid to come. But if she'd gone to Agent Tucker, Sal would probably have been picked up for questioning, and he'd deny knowing anything. She was certain no amount of threatening would get him to rat on his sister. In a moment of desperation, she'd designated herself a temporary undercover agent. She'd get whatever information she could and pass it along to the authorities.

It was a risk. Sal and his sister could have masterminded Scott's abduction. Maybe he planned to get them lost, then abandon them while they left the country. As chilly as the nights were getting, and as far from civilization as they apparently were, they'd die of exposure and starvation before anyone could find them. Jennie shuddered and huddled deeper inside Megan's jacket, thankful she'd thought to use it instead of the lightweight summer jacket she'd brought.

Get real, McGrady. Sal is just protecting Crystal. They'd have no reason to take Scott—at least none that she knew of.

"Okay, hug the left side of the road." Sal pointed off to the right. "There's a steep drop-off coming up. Sometimes the road gets a little rough."

"A little rough?" Megan grabbed the seat for support. "It's been a *little* rough." The truck hit a deep rut, throwing them forward, then back again.

"Sheesh." Algie braked. "You don't expect me to drive over that."

Jennie peered through the windshield at a rock the size of Connecticut. The entire road had been obliterated by tons of rock and debris. "There's no way. We'd better turn around and go back."

"Must have been a rock slide," Sal said. "But you got four-wheel drive, don't you? I've seen trucks on television go over a lot more rugged terrain than this."

"I got news for you, pal—"

"I know, I know," Sal chuckled. "I was teasing. We can walk the rest of the way. It's not that far."

Jennie could have trounced him. He was entirely too happy about the prospect. "How far is it?"

"About half a mile." He turned back to Algie. "Hey, buddy, you better grab the cell phone. I have to call Crystal and let her know where we are."

Algie handed Sal the phone. While he made a call, Algie climbed in the back, opened the lid on the metal box, and pulled out a lantern. Handing it to Kyle, he dove into the box again, this time coming up with a flashlight. "We might want to take the emergency pack too—just in case."

"Definitely." Jennie offered to carry it since she was the only one with first-aid training.

"Sounds good to me." Algie held it out while she slipped the straps over her arms.

"Hey, sis," Sal said into the cell phone. "Yeah. We're on our way. Don't worry. No one followed us." He told Crystal about the rockslide and said they'd be walking in. "See you in a few." He signed off and handed the phone to Algie.

"Everybody ready?" Sal's grin was back.

Jennie zipped up her jacket. "Let's go."

Sal and Kyle led the way with the lantern. Jennie and Lisa stuck close behind them, while Algie and Megan brought up the rear. The enormous darkness seemed to swallow their meager lights. Jennie was glad of the dark. Sal had informed them that the precipice over which they were climbing dropped some two hundred feet into a gorge. They scaled the thirty-foot-wide slide area, climbed over two fallen cedars, then picked up the road on the other side. Once past the slide, she shoved her icicle fingers into her pockets to warm them. During the walk they'd shifted into pairs. Jennie and Sal, with Sal now holding the lantern, walked in front. Kyle and Lisa had apparently decided they had a lot in common and were talking about her dad's career as an airline pilot. Kyle was taking flying lessons.

"Sal"—Jennie felt around for the right button and turned on the tape recorder—"I'm curious. Why doesn't your sister want to talk to the police?"

He shrugged his shoulders. "She is not a criminal, if that's what you think."

"Is she an animal rights activist?"

Sal held the light higher. "She hasn't done anything wrong."

They were back to square one. If Crystal hadn't done anything wrong, why didn't she want to talk to the police? Why was she afraid of being followed? She gave up on that line of questioning. "You seem to know your way around. You must come up here a lot."

"We camped up here once this summer."

"Once? Are you sure you know where you're going?"

"Are you kidding?" He stopped and leaned forward, searching for something. "Crystal gave good directions so, yeah, we'll find it."

"Directions. That means you don't know where she is?"

"I know—sort of."

"What do you mean, sort of?" Jennie didn't like Sal's evasive answers and had the uneasy feeling they might be walking into a trap.

"Hold up, everybody." Sal stopped. "I think this is it."

"If *this* is it," Algie said, joining him, "we're in trouble. I don't see anything that looks or smells remotely like a campsite."

"I hope we're not lost." Lisa's voice held the concern they all felt.

Sal moved to the side of the road, eyeing a white flag that had been tied to the top of a small pine tree.

The rustling of brush nearby startled Jennie. "Listen."

"Probably a possum or something," Kyle said.

Lisa grabbed his arm. "Are you sure? It sounds bigger than that."

Sal laughed. "You guys need to relax."

The rustling grew in intensity, as did Jennie's nerves. "It's hard to relax when your guide doesn't know where he's going."

"He's only following orders." The voice cut through the darkness.

Lisa screamed. Jennie's heart jumped to her throat—more from the scream than from the figure coming toward them. She'd already figured the flag meant that someone would meet them and escort them the rest of the way to the camp.

"Are you sure no one followed you?" Crystal emerged from the dense woods and entered their circle of light. Only then did Jennie panic. She wore a heavy camouflage jacket, fatigues, and combat boots. A strap over her shoulder held a rifle.

"What have you done with Scott?" Jennie moved toward her.

"He's safe. Sal, you stay here with the others. Jennie, come with me."

"No!" Lisa stepped between Jennie and Crystal. "Jennie, you can't go alone. I won't let you."

"Suit yourself." Crystal started to walk away.

"Wait!" Jennie grabbed Crystal's arm, pulling her back around. "Why can't we all go?"

"We're not running an open house. You come alone, Jennie, or you don't see Scott at all." Crystal's eyes shimmered in the light of the kerosene lamp. She looked different than she had at the hospital, and it wasn't just the uniform.

"Why did you take Scott from the hospital?"

Crystal glanced at the others. "That's not open for discussion—not here. If Scott chooses to tell you, that will be up to him."

Jennie couldn't honestly say why, but she trusted Crystal. She still read kindness and compassion in the young woman's eyes.

"Don't, Jennie," Lisa pleaded. "Remember the neo-nazi group. They were going to kill you."

Crystal frowned. "Neo-nazis?"

"It's a long story. This radical group kidnapped me thinking they could make an exchange with the police for the leader's brother. All in all it was a pretty terrifying experience."

"I can imagine. You don't need to worry about us. We wouldn't hurt any of you. We're not violent people."

"Then why are you carrying a rifle?" Jennie asked.

"Protection." She adjusted the strap. "Are you coming?"

"Yes."

"Just for the record, Jennie McGrady, I think you're crazy." Lisa let go of her hand.

"Maybe so, but I have to talk to Scott." Jennie gave Lisa a hug and whispered, "Call Tess," in her ear. "I'll be back."

"Be careful." Lisa reluctantly let her go.

"Come on," Sal said. "Let's build a fire while we're waiting."

Jennie sent a silent plea to God for safety as she turned her back on her friends and followed Crystal into the woods.

Your curiosity is going to get you in big trouble someday, Jennie, her mother had often said. The words had proven true about a dozen times too many. Now, however, Jennie didn't believe she was walking into danger. Scott wouldn't let anything happen to her—if he could help it. That was the scary part about this clandestine meeting. What if she had read Crystal wrong? What if they were holding him hostage? Suppose he had information they wanted. What better way to get it out of him than to threaten to harm her?

You've been reading too many mysteries. She had an opportunity to learn what had happened to Scott and couldn't pass that up. Maybe she could be instrumental in helping Tess and Agent Tucker with their investigation. She backed out of the worrisome thoughts, concentrating instead on putting one foot in front of the other. The road had deteriorated even more with deep ruts filled with muddy water left over from yesterday's rain. "How did you get in here with that slide across the road?"

"That happened this morning."

"So you're trapped back here?"

"There are ways to get around it."

They walked in silence for several minutes before Jennie spoke again. She had a score to settle with Crystal, and this was as good a time as any to bring it up. "Last night, when you took Scott out of the hospital, did you put something in the tea you gave me?"

She looked stricken. "No, of course not. I didn't even know we were leaving until after I'd given it to you."

"Then how could I have slept so soundly?"

"People do, you know. You were exhausted. The tea must have relaxed you enough to help you fall asleep, and once you were out . . ."

"What about the guard? Tess said she'd posted a volunteer deputy outside his door. They found him in an alley outside a bar this morning."

"I'm not surprised."

"So you did drug him."

"We didn't drug anyone. Jeff happens to have a weakness for alcohol. He's a binge drinker—been that way since high school. All we had to do was tell him we'd watch Scott while he had a couple of drinks. It isn't the first time he's passed out."

"I still don't see how you could have gotten Scott out without anyone knowing it."

"We are very adept at getting in and out of places. Besides, there was only one other nurse working with me that night."

"Did you erase his records?" Jennie ducked under a low-hanging branch.

"No. They were not erased. Just misplaced. They show he'd been discharged."

"You said 'we.' Who are you working with?"

Crystal sighed. "I'd rather not say any more, Jennie. I know how odd this must seem to you, but I think you'll understand better when you're able to talk with Scott. He's hoping you'll join us."

When pigs fly. Jennie kept the comment to herself. Scott knew perfectly well that she'd never join a group like ARM. While she agreed with parts of their agenda in protecting animals from abuse, she would never go along with releasing mink or fire-bombing places that served meat. ARM worked outside the law and made up their own rules. He must know she'd never go along with their tactics.

What was Scott up to? Had he seen an opportunity to continue his work with the FBI? Did he need her help? Or was he, as Agent Tucker suggested, a double agent?

Jennie could smell the smoke from a campfire now. A flame flickered through the trees not twenty feet ahead.

In the light cast by the fire, she could see the outline of a building. The red truck parked next to it ignited the fear in her and sent flames shooting into every pore. *Oh, McGrady. What have you gotten yourself into?*

18

"That's Sutherland's truck, isn't it?" Jennie peered at the right front fender but saw no signs of damage.

"What of it?" Crystal seemed more defensive now, wary.

"Did you steal it?"

"Not exactly."

"You can't steal something that belongs to you, Jennie." A familiar voice seemed to come out of the fire.

Jennie narrowed her focus to the shadowed figure standing just outside the fire's light. Remembering Christine's visit to Crystal's house, she ventured a guess. "Mrs. Sutherland?"

"Hardly." The woman came closer to the fire, allowing Jennie a better look. "Mother isn't exactly the ARM type."

"No, I suppose not." Aleshia hadn't seemed the type either. Now, however, dressed in fatigues like the others, she had a cool, calculating air about her that made Jennie realize she was capable of anything—including murder. "The police are looking for you."

"Are they? Why?"

"In connection with your father's death."

"What are you talking about? My father isn't dead. He's missing. He . . ." Aleshia's lower lip began to tremble.

"He's dead. And Jim was arrested." Jennie told her about Jim finding the body and then confessing. "He did it to protect you."

"He's an idiot."

"He saw the fox carcass your father had been skinning when he died and thinks you killed him."

Aleshia lowered her head and closed her eyes. "God help me,

I came close. I don't think I've ever been so angry in my life."

"What happened?"

"After I saw you that morning, I went into town to see Crystal. We had a print job to finish for ARM. We finished there early, and I still had over an hour before I was to meet Mom at the restaurant. I went back out to the farm hoping to talk to Dad about planning a surprise party for my mother's birthday. When I got there, Mom was already gone, and Dad was in the shop. When I saw that he had killed Sasha, I about went crazy. I wanted to kill him."

"But you didn't."

"No. When I asked how he could do such a hateful thing, he turned his back on me and said he had more important things to do than waste his time talking to a turncoat daughter." Aleshia raised clenched fists. "I hit him in the back. I wanted to beat him senseless. I knocked him down. Must have hurt his back again. When I saw the pained expression on his face . . . I, um—I guess the anger sort of drained right out of me. I felt sorry for him, you know. When I left, I ran into Jim in the driveway and told him what Dad had done. I also told him if he still wanted to marry me he'd better never talk to my father again. I don't think he did. And now he never will." Her voice collapsed in a sob.

Crystal placed a comforting arm around her friend's shoulders. Aleshia sniffed, raised her head, and dabbed at the moisture in her eyes with a tissue she'd drawn from her pocket. "I'm okay."

Jennie wanted to urge her on but remembered her grandmother's advice about silence. *"Silence opens the door for confession much more quickly than a barrage of questions."*

After a few awkward moments Aleshia spoke again. "Jim walked me back to my car and we drove down to the lake. He held me for a while. He's so sweet that way. When I'd calmed down, he said he had to get back to work. He walked back to the Bergstroms', and I went into town to run some errands and meet Mom."

"Your dad was alive when you left?"

"As far as I know." She sucked in a shaky breath. "No one came while I was there. The only vehicle in the driveway was Dad's truck. It must have been right after—unless—someone was hiding in the barns. I suppose that's possible."

"Jim could have gone back to the shop and killed him after you left," Jennie said. "Maybe his confession was for real—except that he said he'd put the fox carcass in the freezer, which isn't where the police found it. Someone had thrown it in the trash."

"Why would he do that? It wasn't Jim's fox. It was mine. Besides, a pelt like Sasha's would be worth around sixty-five dollars. There's no way Jim or my father would throw it away."

Jennie puzzled over the information. Who *would* throw away the pelt and why? "Jim could have done it out of anger. I'm sure he didn't like the idea of your father hurting you like that."

Aleshia shook her head. "I can't believe Jim did it."

"Well, someone sure did. One of your ARM buddies, maybe?" Jennie was taking a chance speaking out like that, but she had Aleshia talking now and felt duty bound to press the issue. "They left a mark. An X on his back."

"No. I'll admit there are some fringe groups who affiliate themselves with ARM that could be responsible, but I seriously doubt that. You see, Jennie, when any of our members commit a humane act like releasing animals or protesting furriers, we do it for the love of animals. We want the world to know that we are responsible. Our members send communications to our spokesperson, who is not involved in the fieldwork. He works directly with the media. Since he's only responsible for passing along information, he's not involved in any kind of criminal activity. I know no one from ARM did it because if they had, there would have been a memo admitting responsibility."

Crystal placed a hand on Jennie's arm. "Aleshia is right. As I said before, our credo is to protect animals, not to kill. Sometimes we're embarrassed by the violent acts of people who claim to be part of ARM. Like any group we have our share of loose cannons who see ARM as a license to commit terrible crimes."

Jennie didn't see anything humane in releasing mink. "What about the mink that died as a result of being released? Do you consider that humane?"

"It's a tragedy to lose any animal, of course, but we believe many of them will survive."

This wasn't the time to debate the issue. They were convinced that what they were doing was noble and somehow above the law.

But she hadn't come here to argue. She hadn't seen Scott yet and that worried her. "You said Scott was here."

"He is." Aleshia nodded toward the stone building. "He's asleep."

"I gave him some pain pills about an hour ago," Crystal said. "It's good he's resting. He'll need strength for the trip tomorrow."

"Trip? Where are you going?"

Crystal removed the gun, which was still slung over her shoulder, and placed it in the back of the truck. "Until Scott is able to make it on his own, we need to protect him from the police and whoever is trying to kill him. That means we must keep moving."

"That's the big question, isn't it?" Jennie stepped closer to the fire, holding out her hands to warm them. "Who tried to kill Scott? Personally, I think it's the same person who killed Mr. Sutherland."

"I think so too." Aleshia picked up a stick and stirred the fire. "This is why we know it couldn't have been any of our people. While some ARM members might be capable of such a thing, they would never harm another member."

Unless someone in the group discovered he wasn't really one of them. Jennie couldn't voice the thought. Aleshia and Crystal apparently believed Scott to be a member. Which made little or no sense. If a member of ARM had discovered Scott's duplicity, wouldn't he or she have warned the others?

Aleshia pulled a Thermos from the back of the truck, which was apparently where they kept their supplies, and poured something hot and steamy into a cup, then brought it to Jennie. "Here. You might as well relax."

Jennie took the cup. Hot chocolate. She sipped at it, letting the steamy heat warm her hands and face. "I can't stay too long. My friends will be wondering what happened to me. Besides, it's getting late. Megan's parents will be worried."

"It's only nine." Aleshia poured a cup from another Thermos and handed it to Crystal. She lowered herself to a log near the fire. She looked sad and almost vulnerable. Jennie felt sorry for her. She'd lost her father, and her fiancé had branded himself the killer.

Her gaze shifted from the fire to Jennie. "Scott says you may be able to help us find the person who tried to run him down."

"I don't see how." Jennie sat on the other end of Aleshia's log. "To tell you the truth, you were my main suspect. Jim was next. I'm not sure where to go from there."

"Well, I didn't do it. Neither did Jim."

Jennie looked at the two women sharing the same fire with her. One a nurse, the other a fashion designer. "How did you come to join ARM?"

"Me or Crystal?"

"Both of you."

"We got involved our first year of college," Crystal said. "I have always loved animals. In fact, I'm going back to school this winter. I'm getting my degree in veterinary medicine."

Aleshia smiled at that. "Crystal and I used to release mink when we were kids. I've always hated what my parents did for a living. When you're a kid, you don't have much say. Not that my father ever listened to me. He was always disappointed that I didn't share his views. But I did gain a tremendous satisfaction in releasing one or two mink at a time. We'd wait until pelting season when he was too busy to notice."

"I don't think he ever caught on," Crystal said, "In college, we met a couple who told us about ARM. Their philosophy was so much like ours, we thought we'd like to join."

"How do you join? I mean, is there an application or—"

"Oh no. Nothing like that." Aleshia leaned forward and added another log to the fire. "Basically you declare yourself a member and start working on whatever needs doing. Once you've made a hit or done something significant, you let headquarters know."

"Is there an office or something?"

"No, that would be too dangerous. I've heard that Sonja has a command center, but no one knows where it is. She—or he— moves around a lot. Most of us work out of our homes. We communicate via e-mail and change our addresses frequently."

"But you don't. You've been in the same area since—what?"

"Aleshia's been here all her life. My parents came in as migrant workers when I was twelve. We liked the area and decided to settle here. We've never been in on the kinds of activity that could land us in jail. My affiliation with ARM is a secret. Aleshia is the only one around here who admits to being a member."

"That was to goad my father. Sometimes I protest or march, but I don't actually take part in the raids—neither does Crystal. We act as an information network for the Northwest. We put out an underground newspaper and distribute flyers eliciting support for the cause. It's all legal under the First Amendment."

"Taking a patient out of the hospital is not legal."

"We didn't take him. Scott wanted to go," Crystal said. "We just made it possible."

"Tell me what happened at the hospital. You said earlier you would." Jennie stretched her long legs out in front of her, amazed that she was beginning to feel comfortable with the two women she'd earlier branded as terrorists and possible killers.

"Scott is a member of ARM. He'd asked a fellow ARM member in Florida to set him up with members in the area. She contacted us to let us know he was coming."

"Melissa?"

Crystal's eyes widened in surprise. "You know her?"

"I met her through Scott when I was in Florida."

"Small world. Anyway, Melissa e-mailed us that Scott would be coming to scope out some of the farms in the area."

"Scott said he didn't know you, Aleshia," Jennie said.

"He didn't. Our only contact was through e-mail using code names. Scott and I didn't actually meet until after he was in the hospital. Crystal recognized his name and called me. We told him who we were, and he asked us to help him escape."

"I wish he'd have told me. I imagined all sorts of things." Anger stirred inside her. She'd been worried sick about the jerk. What bothered her most was that he hadn't trusted her.

"He wanted to wake you, but we convinced him it was too risky." Aleshia straightened and stretched, rubbing her side. "He's a great guy, Jennie. Very dedicated. Melissa couldn't say enough good things about him."

That struck Jennie as odd. Hadn't Scott told Melissa he was leaving ARM because of his friend's death? If Jennie were Melissa, she'd have been suspicious and would have imparted those suspicions along with a warning to the other members. However, if the FBI set Scott up out here, could they have used Melissa's name? Could they have forced her to send the correspondence—

or had they arrested her? Jennie's head swam with possibilities.

"According to Melissa," Crystal said, "Scott is one of our most dedicated members. In fact, I wouldn't be surprised if he turned out to be Sonja."

"That's pure speculation. We'll never know for sure." Aleshia stood and said, "I'll go check on our patient."

Minutes later, Scott emerged from the cabin on crutches. "Why didn't you tell me Jennie was here?"

Jennie rose and took a step toward him. She had so many questions yet feared asking any of them in case he really was gathering information for the FBI.

"Hey, Jen."

"Hey. You look good for someone who's been hit by a truck."

He smiled. "Thanks, I think." He quickly closed the distance between them and opened his arms to her. Jennie stepped into them. Resting her head against his shoulder, they held each other. He felt so good and warm and solid, Jennie could have cried.

"I've missed you." His crutches fell to the ground, and he leaned heavily on her for support.

Jennie leaned over and picked them up. "I think you have some explaining to do."

"Come on." He tucked the tops of the crutches back under his arms and moved to the log Jennie had been sitting on. Looking back at his cohorts, he said, "Could you give us a few minutes?"

"Sure. We need to scrounge up more firewood anyway," Aleshia said. Taking a flashlight from the back of the truck, they headed into the woods.

Jennie waited until they were gone, then whispered, "What's going on with you? They think you're Sonja. Whose side are you on, anyway? I was all ready to believe you in the hospital."

Scott leaned over and kissed her.

Jennie backed away. "What was that for?"

"To shut you up." His arm went around her, pulling her close. In a voice so soft she could hardly hear, he said, "I had to get out of the hospital. I'm close, Jennie. I don't know who killed Sutherland, but I know why. When I stopped by to see how he was doing that day after I left you, he said he'd found evidence that would destroy ARM. Said something about going to the source. I think he knew who Sonja was."

"Do you think Sonja killed him?"

"I'd bet on it. Sutherland wasn't very discreet. If he told me, chances are he mentioned it to others as well. I tried to get him to tell me more, but he just got mad again. I left and checked into a motel over by the freeway. That afternoon I got a call from a guy who said he knew who Sonja was and told me to meet him at Arnie's Café in town. I never got there. I figure he was waiting for me by the side of the road. I don't remember much more than seeing the headlights of a truck coming straight at me."

"If he called you at the hotel, he must have followed you from Sutherlands'. Did anyone see you talking to him?"

"I don't think so. When I got to the farm, there wasn't anyone else around. I didn't check at the house, just went straight down to the shop. I suppose Christine could have been there, but I didn't see her car."

"Whew. Sutherlands' must have been a pretty busy place. You, Aleshia, Jim, Tom, and Mary—I'm going to have to do a timeline to see who was where and when." Lowering her voice again she added, "Aleshia says she didn't kill her dad, but I'm not sure I believe her. Are you sure the person who called was a man?"

"It was a deep voice, but now that you mention it, it sounded odd—like it had been distorted."

"Sonja." Jennie turned around to look at the red truck. "I could be wrong, but I feel like the key to all this is in whoever hit you. You were heading into town. Did the truck hit you head on or from behind?"

"Head on. I tried to swerve, but he kept coming at me."

"So the damage to the truck would be on which side?"

Scott frowned and closed his eyes, apparently running it through his mind again. He opened them. "The left."

Jennie straightened, stepped over the log, then walked around the truck. "There's a dent in the left front fender and the headlight is broken. I'll bet anything this is the truck that hit you."

Scott hobbled over to look.

Rustling noises in the bushes behind them sent Jennie's heart skittering. "We'd better get out of here."

19

"You're not going anywhere." A man stepped out of the bushes. In his jeans, flannel shirt, and utility vest, he looked like a hunter except for the gun—a .38 caliber, similar to the kind her father used. "FBI. Get your hands up where I can see them."

"What's. . . ?" Jennie stammered. "How did you—"

"Are you Jennie McGrady?"

Jennie swallowed hard. "Y-yes."

"Nice going, McGrady." Scott glared at her in disgust. "I thought I could trust you."

"I didn't know—they must have followed me." Exasperated, Jennie lifted her hands above her head. She was more frustrated with herself than with the bureau. She should have known they'd put a tail on Sal—her, too, for that matter.

On the other side of the camp, Aleshia and Crystal came into view, both handcuffed and escorted by three agents, one of them Agent Tucker. The women's angry looks relayed the same message Scott had given her. *Traitor.*

Jennie couldn't bear to look at Scott for fear of seeing his anger. She wished there were something she could do. She listened helplessly while the agents read them their rights.

Agent Tucker whipped out a radio and mumbled something into it about coming in. Part of her was glad the agents had come. Now that she'd seen the damage to Sutherland's truck, she wasn't so sure about Aleshia's innocence. On the other hand, she felt certain Scott had nothing to do with the murder and couldn't bear to think she'd been to blame for his arrest. What worried her even more was what they planned to do with her.

"It's a good thing they followed us," Jennie said to Scott. "By the looks of that truck, Aleshia's the one who hit you."

"What are you talking about?" Aleshia glanced from Scott to Jennie.

"The headlight is broken and there's a dent on the left fender. You used it to run Scott down, didn't you? You left him for dead. When he showed up at the hospital, Crystal called to tell you your efforts had failed. Then you had to convince him to leave the hospital with you. He played right into your hands."

Aleshia shook her head. "You're crazy. I have no idea how the dent got there."

"Sure. And you have no idea how your father ended up in the gas chamber either."

"That's right." Aleshia collapsed in a sob. "I didn't kill him. I didn't even take the truck until three this morning. It had a bunk in the canopy, and I thought it would be more comfortable for Scott than the back of my car. You have to believe me."

"Where were you last night when Crystal called?" Jennie asked.

"Where do you get off asking me questions? I don't have to tell you anything."

"Aleshia," Crystal said, "it's better to tell them. We have nothing to hide." Turning to Jennie she said, "She was at home."

"Where is Aleshia's car?" Agent Tucker asked before Jennie had a chance.

"Parked in a campground near here," Crystal answered. "Off the main road. Aleshia picked Scott and me up at the hospital in the truck. My car is still in the hospital lot."

"I had Crystal drop me off at the farm to pick up my car," Aleshia said finally. "I met them at the campground and rode up here with them in the truck."

Tucker signaled one of the agents, asking him to check the truck for prints. The accusations Jennie had made left Scott and Crystal looking stunned. Aleshia's face still held an expression of disbelief.

The tape recorder in Jennie's pocket clicked off. The small noise was almost deafening in the silence.

"What was that?" the agent holding her and Scott at gunpoint demanded.

"A tape recorder." Jennie had done nothing wrong yet felt enormous guilt.

Tucker approached her, hand extended. "Let's have it."

While she had planned from the start to give the tape to the agent, she did it now with reluctance.

"You recorded us?" Crystal stood there openmouthed. "How could you do that?"

Aleshia set her jaw. "This is your fault, Chambers. You told us we could trust her. I expected better of you. I'll get you for this. I don't know how, but I will."

"No one's getting anyone." Tucker pocketed the tape recorder and nodded at the other agents. "Get them into town. Jennie, you come with me. I'll drive Sutherland's truck. Miss Sutherland, I trust you have the keys."

Aleshia tipped her head back. "You want them, you can get them yourself."

"Aleshia," Crystal gently prodded, "we should cooperate. We haven't done anything wrong. Let's not push it."

"Smart lady. You'll do well to listen to your friend. Now, let's try this again. Where are the keys?"

"They're in the ignition."

The agent sent to get prints off the truck's interior backed out of the driver's side. "I'm finished. I lifted several sets of prints off the wheel and dash."

"Okay, let's go," Tucker said.

One of the agents prodded Scott to move ahead.

"Wait!" Jennie yelled. "You're not going to make him walk out, are you? Can't you see his leg is in a cast?"

"Relax, kid. It's only for a few feet." While the agent spoke, a huge truck with a camouflage canopy rumbled in.

"Your friends will go in that," Tucker said.

"Can't I go with them? I'd like a chance to explain."

"No." Tucker took the agent with Scott aside. "I'll take Jennie to the Bergstroms' and meet you at the sheriff's office."

The agents instructed Aleshia, Crystal, and Scott to get into the back of the truck. Two agents climbed in back with the prisoners, while two sat up front. When they'd gone, Tucker doused the fire, loaded up the truck with camp stuff that was lying around, and helped Jennie into the cab of the Sutherlands' truck.

They rode in silence for several minutes before Jennie finally spoke. "You didn't have to follow me," she said. "I was perfectly safe."

"Were you?" He glanced at her, his features stern and unyielding in the dim glow of the dashboard lights.

"They trusted me. They trusted Scott. He was trying to—"

"Avoid arrest?"

"He was afraid you wouldn't believe him. He's still on your side."

"Do you know that for sure?"

Jennie heaved a heavy sigh and leaned her head against the window. Fairly certain wouldn't cut it. "If you were worried about me, why did you let me go into the camp? Why didn't you stop us at the slide?"

"You don't want to know."

"What—did you lose us?"

He gave her a half smile and shook his head. "Flat tire. By the time we caught up with your friends, you were already gone. We sent them home and had to find another way in. Took us a while to locate the camp. Agent Conner had you in his sights the whole time but was ordered not to go in until he had backup—unless he could see that you were in imminent danger."

"I still think you shouldn't have arrested them. Scott says he was close to finding out who Sonja is. He thinks Sonja was the one who hit him."

"He may be right. Even if we find he's being straight with us, we can't let him stay out here. It's not safe for him to be on the case anymore. Someone is on to him. The word is out to ARM members that Scott is working with the FBI."

"So you're arresting Scott for his own protection?"

"We're taking him to a safe location until we can sort this out."

Jennie's shoulders sagged with relief. "I just thought of something. If Aleshia ran Scott down, she must have already known he wasn't one of them. Only—she didn't act like she knew. Neither did Crystal. And if they did, wouldn't they have done something about Scott before now? When I saw the condition of this truck, I automatically suspected Aleshia, but now that I think about it, it doesn't seem likely. They were both really nice to me. Scott told them to let me come in to see him, and they did. I think they totally believed Scott was one of them. They talked openly with me and made it clear that they stayed away from anything illegal."

"Crystal and Aleshia might be *nice*, Jennie. Unfortunately, they have a warped sense of justice. For them the ends justify the means. They believe they're innocent as long as they aren't actively participating in the raids or the fires or the bombings. But they write about it. They make the terrorists sound like heroes."

"Maybe so, but some of their ideas are good. They want to protect animals from abuse."

"Humph. Jennie, you could have a dozen eggs and all of them except one could be okay. But if you toss the rotten egg in with the good, you taint all of them. They walk a fine line, and I wouldn't be a bit surprised if one or both of them hadn't crossed over it. You're forgetting, too, that these girls aren't working alone. It's entirely possible Aleshia ordered the hit on Scott and on her father."

He was right. Their dedication to ARM and their near worship of the leader tainted their lives. Still, thinking back to the way Aleshia and Crystal had talked to her, she couldn't quite see them killing anyone.

"If you plan on going into law enforcement, you're going to have to get a little tougher on crime."

"Not everything is clear cut. There are gray areas," Jennie defended.

"You got that right. Too many holes."

"Are you any closer to figuring out who killed Mr. Sutherland?"

He shook his head. "Are you?"

She laughed at that. "I've got some ideas."

"Well, let's hear them."

Jennie sneaked a look at him to see whether or not he was serious. He caught her glance and said, "Go ahead."

"I think we need to reconstruct that morning before Mr. Sutherland turned up missing. Seems like he had a lot of people coming and going. Scott stopped to talk to him. Tom dropped by to see how his back was doing. Of course, I'm sure neither of them did it, so it would have to have been one of the others. Christine said she left at ten-thirty to go shopping. Aleshia said she came back shortly after that to talk to her dad about Christine's birthday. She wanted to kill her dad when she saw that he had killed Sasha."

Tucker raised his eyebrows. "Sasha—the fox."

"Right."

"And Aleshia told you all this tonight?"

"Yes. It should all be on the tape. I would have gotten more if you hadn't butted in."

"That's the thanks we get for saving your skin?" He chuckled. "Go on."

"Aleshia said she hit him and pushed him down, then ran into Jim on her way out. They went down to the lake and talked, then she left to meet her mom in town and Jim went home."

"Did she say when she left?"

"At eleven-thirty. Jim could have gone back and killed him. He could be lying about where he'd put the pelt."

"Oh, you think so, huh?" The agent wasn't taking her seriously, but she liked talking it out and trying to clarify things in her own mind.

"It makes sense. If he killed Mr. Sutherland and threw the pelt away, he'd have known the pelt was in the garbage can. He could have lied about where he found it so you'd think he really didn't do it."

He nodded. "Know what I think?"

"What?"

"I think you ought to forget about being a cop and become a mystery writer."

"Well, it's possible—he did have a motive. Mr. Sutherland's cruelty toward Aleshia could have set him off. Maybe he went back to have a showdown with Mr. Sutherland." Jennie sighed, remembering the timetable. "That doesn't work, does it? Like Tom said, Jim wouldn't have had time to do all that. Unless he and Aleshia were in on it together."

"Going back over the parade of people Bob saw that morning

is good thinking. You mentioned Tom. What do you think about him as a suspect?"

"He doesn't have a motive."

"That you know of. Now, if Tom is Sonja, the motive might be as simple as wanting to rid the world of another mink farmer."

"I know you're supposed to look at everyone as a suspect, but somehow I don't see Tom as a killer."

"That your gut feeling?"

"Um—yeah, I guess it is. Or maybe it's that I've known them for years."

"Everyone can be provoked to anger. Given the right circumstances, anyone could kill. I suspect whoever killed Sutherland did so in a fit of rage. There doesn't necessarily need to be a reason other than that."

"Yes, but . . . shouldn't you look at motives just the same? Like who stands to profit the most from Mr. Sutherland's death? There must be an insurance policy. Does Mrs. Sutherland stand to get a lot of money?"

"We're way ahead of you there, Jennie. In fact, in an investigation like this, the wife is often the first person of interest. The policy isn't a big one—pays off the mortgage on the house and gives her seventy-five thousand dollars cash. Christine gets the business, of course, but it was already hers since they had joint ownership. She's not thrilled about that—means she'd have to run it herself. Aleshia isn't about to help. She's planning to sell."

"Really? Seems awfully soon."

"It's not that unusual. Widows often sell—too many memories. You have to admit it's a pretty big operation for a woman like Christine."

"I suppose so. Still, she could hire another person besides Stan." Saying Stan's name sent Jennie's thoughts in another direction. She reigned them in to listen to Agent Tucker.

"What I find even more interesting is that Tom wants to buy the place. If you were looking for motive on Tom's part—that might be it."

"I don't believe that for one minute. I was just thinking—wasn't Stan the one who called in to report that Sutherland was missing?"

"That's right."

"Maybe he went to tell Mr. Sutherland he had to leave for a few days. Mr. Sutherland wouldn't have been too happy about that. Suppose he got mad at Stan . . . after all, Stan was out in the barns when the raid took place. He could have had a fight with Mr. S. and killed him, then called the sheriff."

Tucker agreed that might be a possibility. He glanced into the rearview mirror and frowned. "That's odd."

Jennie turned around, her gaze settling on the headlights coming up behind them. "Are they following us?"

"Could be. I noticed them a ways back. There's not much traffic out here. We still haven't hit the freeway. Of course, there are some homes out in this area, so it could be a local resident."

Although they had left the narrow one-lane road, they were still on a secondary highway with little room for a car to pass. The vehicle was gaining on them, coming too fast for comfort.

Fear rose like bile in the pit of her stomach. She'd been through this sort of thing before—twice, in fact. Once in Florida when a truck slammed into Gram's rental car and it flipped over the railing, plunging them into the treacherous Gulf waters near Dolphin Island. The other was on the coast highway when she was forced off the road over a cliff. She'd survived both with only minor injuries, but they say the third time is a charm.

A charm. Right. *This time, though, you're in a truck,* she reminded herself.

"Whoever it is seems to be in a hurry." Tucker pulled off onto the shoulder, and the car passed. Air hissed through Jennie's teeth.

Tucker gave her an odd look, shifted, and drove on. "What's with the panic attack?"

Jennie told him about her near misses. "I was afraid this would be another one."

He smiled. "I can see why you'd be a little nervous. No need to worry about that one, though. Probably just a local."

"Right."

Tucker pulled the tape out of his pocket and plugged it into the truck's tape player. "Might as well see what you've got on this."

What she had was static and not much else. "It's awful. The

stupid thing didn't pick up anything expect my jacket moving against it."

"I'm not surprised. Tape recorders like this aren't very good for surveillance. Next time, get a better-quality machine. Better yet, talk to us before you head out on your own. It's not a big loss, though. From what you told me they didn't leak any top-secret information."

"That's true." Jennie couldn't decide if Agent Tucker was amusing himself at her expense or if he really was interested in her observations. Leaning comfortably against the seat again, she picked up the thread she'd been following earlier. "So what do you think about Stan as a suspect?"

"Bears checking into. Holy—" Tucker slammed on the brakes.

A wall of flames exploded in front of them. The truck skidded on the slick pavement, went into a spin, and headed straight for a tree.

20

"Hold on!" Agent Tucker yanked the wheel to the left. The truck spun, tipping wildly.

Too terrified to scream, Jennie pressed her feet to the floor, her hands to the dash. She closed her eyes but couldn't shut off the sound of screeching tires or the caustic smell of smoke and gasoline.

She opened her eyes again and wished she hadn't. The fire was to their left now, flames rolling and fierce, reminding Jennie of something out of a James Bond movie. They'd spun almost full circle. Tucker's correction caused them to miss the trees, but not the waterfall or the solid rock wall behind it. The truck lurched forward into the ditch, then crashed into the rocks.

The windshield shattered. An airbag exploded out of its nest, slamming Jennie against the seat. Almost instantly the taut bag went limp, hanging out like a tongue. Jennie dropped forward, straining against the seat belt. If not for the belt, she'd have fallen against Agent Tucker.

The air bags left behind a blast of white dust. Jennie's lungs burned, and she and Tucker began coughing. She'd heard somewhere that the dust was a propellant and very caustic. Jennie rolled down the window to let in some air. The dust began to settle, making the air inside the cabin more breathable.

The truck had hit the rocks at an angle with the driver's side taking the hardest blow. The waterfall's relentless surge pounded against the windshield, pouring through a six-inch hole and dousing the cab and its occupants with chilling mountain water.

Tucker grunted as he tried to extricate himself from the seat belt. "You okay, Jennie?" He spoke through gritted teeth as though he was in a great deal of pain.

"I . . . I think so. How about you?" She reached up and felt around the dome light for a switch. She breathed a sigh of relief when it came on.

"Not so good. My shoulder's hurt. Legs . . . are pinned under here. Can't move. Looks like my door is jammed shut. Can you get out?"

"I'm not sure." Jennie pulled the handle back and pushed. Her strength proved no match for the heavy door and the gravity that seemed to add another hundred pounds of pressure. She managed to open it a few inches. It slammed back, nearly trapping her fingers in its metal grip. "It's too heavy. I'll have to climb out the window."

"Wait—see if you can find the cell phone."

Find the cell phone. Check Tucker for injuries. Stop the water. A list of things she needed to do ran in her head. There were far too many. Jennie's hand shook as she sought to release the seat belt. *Cell phone first. Call for help.*

Jennie felt like a monkey hanging on to whatever secure device she could find, then bracing and balancing herself so she wouldn't fall against Tucker. Hanging upside down, she managed to locate the cell phone. "It's wedged under the brake," Jennie panted.

"Can you get it out?"

"Your foot's in the way."

"Which one?"

"Right."

Tucker gritted his teeth and tried to move it. "No use. It won't budge. Shove my foot out of the way."

"I don't want to move it."

"Don't argue," he gasped. "Just do it."

Jennie sucked in a deep breath, pulling gently at first, then harder. She could almost feel Tucker's pain as he cried out. With tears in her eyes, she retrieved the cell phone and lifted if out of the pink-tinged water. "You're bleeding. I need to—"

"No. Call first."

"I don't even know where we are."

"Tell them we're—" He groaned again and passed out.

A small noise escaped through the hand she'd pressed to her mouth to keep from screaming. *Calm down, McGrady. You can do this. You are not going to cry. You are going to get help.* She concentrated on taking several long, deep breaths while she punched in 9-1-1.

In a voice surprisingly strong and edged with panic, she told the operator what had happened.

"Can you give me a landmark, anything to help us locate you?"

"We're still in the mountains," she said, "on Highway 20, near Tombstone Summit. Agent Tucker is trapped inside." The cell phone cut in and out, then went dead.

Jennie hit it against her hand, trying to revive it. Water must have seeped into the components. She threw it down and turned back to Tucker. He was still alive. Only he wouldn't be for long. Jennie offered up a continual prayer as she went to work. If she could focus on one thing at a time, she'd be okay.

Water still poured through the broken windshield. It was knee high now. The icy water should slow down and maybe even stop the bleeding in Tucker's leg. Jennie rolled down her window, then braced herself again. Within a few seconds she was standing on the ground. Her legs felt like shifting sand. She held on to the door handle for support.

The fire had burned itself out and was no longer a threat. Someone had deliberately sabotaged them, pouring gas all over the road, then torching it. From the volume of flames, Jennie suspected it had been set off by a fire bomb. She brought her thoughts up short. *Don't think about that now. Got to help Agent Tucker.*

Climbing back inside the cab, she rescued a flashlight from the backpack Algie had given her. She'd taken it off and set it at her feet for the ride home. Now she set it on the seat, out of the water, then climbed back outside.

She rummaged around in the back of the truck until she found a plastic tarp. Jennie then spread it across the windshield and secured it as best she could, tying the ends to the side mirrors and right front bumper.

The truck wasn't tipped as much as she had first thought. The running board on the passenger side was buried in dirt, but there wasn't much clearance for the door. If the damage to the fender hadn't jammed it completely, she might be able to open it enough to let the quickly rising water out of the cab. Gripping the door handle with both hands, she yanked it open.

"Yes!" Water squeezed through the narrow opening, creating a waterfall of its own. Two small victories. Jennie felt like cheering, but there wasn't time.

Back inside the cab, she checked the survival pack again, this time pulling out an emergency blanket. Jennie arranged it around Agent Tucker the best she could.

He groaned when she touched him. "What—"

"It's okay. I called 9–1–1. They're on their way right now." Jennie added an *I hope* but didn't say it aloud.

"Good girl. You need to call Tess—have her tell the others—" He coughed and spasmed in pain.

"Don't try to talk. The cell phone isn't working. But don't worry. As soon as the rescue unit gets here, I'll call."

"Umm." His eyes drifted closed.

"I stopped the water and found a blanket for you." Her teeth were starting to chatter, and her fingers had gone numb, but she couldn't quit now. "I'm going to see if I can get you out."

Using the flashlight, she examined the area pinning his legs. She shrank back at the mutilated, twisted wreckage that held his legs in a vice. There was no way she could free him. Gritting her teeth, she moved forward again, searching for the source of the bleeding. She could see the torn flesh on his knee, but the way he was pinned in, she couldn't get at it to apply a dressing. At least there was no blood dripping from it now. It was no use. She couldn't even get in to check the other leg for injuries.

Frustrated, Jennie left the cab again. Nearly everything she did seemed to raise the awful dust, causing her to cough again. She rubbed her hands together to warm them, ran in place, then jogged in a widening circle. She needed to keep moving. Her wet jeans stuck to her legs. Her boots sloshed when she walked. The parka had resisted much of the water, so her upper half was relatively dry.

She looked around and found herself standing on the still-warm pavement that had only a short time ago been ablaze. A fire deliberately set to blow them up or send them spiraling off the road.

Jennie remembered the car that had passed them earlier. Did the person driving it have something to do with ambushing them? Had it been someone from ARM? Were they retaliating against Aleshia and Crystal's arrest? Had someone from ARM followed them as well?

Jennie replayed the horrible moments before the crash. The fireball lighting up the sky. Tucker breaking and careening out of control. The scene flashed through her mind again. For a split second before they'd gone off the road, Jennie had seen something—two red flashes had appeared through the wall of flames. Taillights. She closed her eyes, visualizing them again. While she couldn't be absolutely certain, she thought they might have belonged to the car that had passed only minutes before. Jennie wished she could remember more details. She searched her mind for color, make, model, license, but came up empty. Somewhere in her brain was a picture of it. She just hoped it would reveal itself before it was too late.

Walking back to the truck, she crawled into the back and eventually found the Thermoses of passably warm coffee and cocoa. Using the one remaining lid, she poured a small amount of the chocolate into the cup and took several sips. The activity and adrenaline had warmed her some, and the warm chocolate settled her insides. She drained the chocolate, then took the coffee and cup into the cab for Tucker.

Twenty minutes later Jennie heard sirens. She'd spent the entire time walking up and down the road, checking on Tucker every couple of minutes. The state police arrived first, then a fire-rescue unit. Within half an hour they'd untangled Tucker from the twisted wreckage with the Jaws of Life, stabilized him, and transferred him to the ambulance. Jennie, wrapped in blankets and sitting in the back of the ambulance with Tucker, was still shaking when they took off.

———

"Jennie!" Lisa met her in the emergency room and ran toward her, arms extended.

Megan followed close behind. "Thank God you're okay."

"How did you find out about it?" She hadn't even had a chance to call.

"Tess called, said you were here."

Jennie nodded. She'd already spoken to Tess and given her statement and suspected Tess had gone on to talk to Agent Tucker.

After a quick hug, Lisa backed away wrinkling her nose. "Ugh—your clothes and your hair smell awful."

Jennie brought her sleeve up and sniffed. "Smoke."

"You were in a fire? A forest fire? Tess said it was an accident."

"Oh no . . . did the truck catch fire?" Megan asked.

"No. But someone poured gas on the road and ignited it. Tucker swerved to miss it. We ran into a ditch." She turned to Megan. "Sorry about the jacket—I'll pay to have it cleaned."

"That's not important. I'm just glad you're okay."

"What happened out there?" Lisa asked. "Agent Tucker made us go home. We didn't want to, Jen, but—"

"I'm glad you did. Judging from what happened to Agent Tucker and me, things could have gotten really ugly for everybody out there. I've been trying to figure out how the person who sabotaged us knew we were there. They either had to have followed us out there without the FBI knowing it, or they were meeting Aleshia and Crystal. They could have come in after the FBI was already there and waited until we left. But if that's the case, why didn't they go after the truck carrying the prisoners?" Jennie slipped her jacket off, wincing at the pain in her right shoulder.

"Maybe they did." Lisa unzipped her coat.

"No, Tess would have said. They were after me or Agent Tucker."

"Do you think it was a member of ARM?" Megan helped Jennie remove the jacket and set it on the back of a chair.

Jennie rubbed her shoulder and tipped her stiff neck side to side. "I'd bet on it."

The doctor came into the cubicle and asked Lisa and Megan to leave while he examined Jennie for injuries. The news was good. She'd escaped with minor bumps and bruises and could expect to be sore for a few days. "If you have any trouble, you give me a call, okay?"

"Sure." Jennie hopped off the stretcher. "How's Agent Tucker doing?"

"Amazingly well. No broken bones. Bump on the head and a nasty-looking knee. We've stitched up the gash in his left leg. Looks like it's mostly soft-tissue damage. He'll be laid up for a day or two, though." The doctor smiled. "By the way, he said to tell you thanks."

"Glad I could help. Can I see him?"

"Nope. He left with the sheriff a few minutes ago."

"Humph. He could have at least said good-bye." Jennie slipped her smelly coat back on and left. Meeting Lisa and Megan, she said, "Let's get out of here. I can't wait to take a shower."

"I can understand why." Lisa tossed Jennie the keys to the Mustang.

"Where are your parents, Megan? I'm surprised they're not down here chewing me out."

"They aren't home. They went into Salem for dinner and a movie. They don't even know we've been gone."

Not home—gone to Salem. Or maybe into the mountains. She had left them a note. Tom and Mary could have followed them. As ludicrous as the idea was, Jennie couldn't help superimposing the picture of the back of Tom and Mary's car over the one imprinted in her mind. A useless exercise. At the moment she couldn't even remember what kind of car they had and didn't think it wise to ask Megan.

"Well," Lisa said expectantly as she buckled the seat belt. "Aren't you going to tell us what happened?"

"We want to hear everything from the minute you left us until we got to the hospital."

Jennie started the car and backed out of the parking space. While she drove, she related all the details she could remember, including Scott's affiliation with the FBI. She wrapped the story up by saying, "That's about it. Aleshia, Crystal, and Scott have all been arrested. Scott's been taken somewhere safe. I hope Agent Tucker at least tells me where so I can see him. Scott thinks I ratted on him."

"I'm sure he'll understand. What about Sal?" Megan asked. "Was he arrested too?"

"Sal?" Jennie eyed Megan in the rearview mirror. "Wasn't he with you?"

"He was at first. When Agent Tucker ordered us out of there, we all left, but we'd only gone a little ways when Sal told Algie to stop the truck and let him out. He said he was going back to the camp to make sure the cops didn't hassle his sister."

"He never showed up. Of course, he could have come in and seen the agents—"

"That means he's still out there somewhere." Megan bit her lower lip. "Maybe he got lost. I'll call Algie when we get home."

"There's another possibility." Jennie tightened her grip on the steering wheel. "Maybe he's the one who ambushed us."

21

"Not Sal," Megan said. "I've known him for a long time. Trust me, he is not into terrorism."

"Did you know Crystal was a member of ARM?" Jennie eased onto the main road and increased her speed.

"N-no, but—"

"People aren't always what they seem."

"I suppose that's true," Megan said, "but you can't go around suspecting everybody."

"No." Jennie frowned. "You have to admit, though, there's plenty of room for it where Sal is concerned. Think about it. He leaves you guys and says he's going to the camp. Only he doesn't show up, and an hour later the truck Agent Tucker and I are riding in is sabotaged."

"He could have gotten lost." Megan folded her arms and rested them on the front seat. "Sal didn't know where the camp was, remember?"

"He must have had an idea or he wouldn't have gone."

"That's true," Lisa said.

"It wouldn't have taken a genius to figure it out. All he would have had to do was follow the trail. He gets to the camp and sees the FBI agents are already there. He hides until they're ready to leave."

"Wait a minute." Lisa tossed back her hair with a head shake. "Let's say he did that—how would he get out after you left? He would have had to walk out."

"True. He could have hitched a ride in the back of Sutherland's truck." Jennie shook her head. "But if he did that he couldn't have been in the car that passed us—unless . . ."

"Unless what?" Lisa asked.

"He could have hidden on the truck as far as the park where Aleshia had parked her car." Jennie brought up the image of Aleshia's Lexus. The car that had passed them had been a dark color, and the taillights could have matched—maybe. "He'd have had to jump out of the truck while it was moving. That doesn't seem likely, but it is a possibility. On the other hand, he could have met someone out there."

"What if he didn't?" Megan gave her a worried look. "What if he's lost out there? What if he did hitch a ride like you said? He could have been hurt in the accident too."

"Well, he wasn't in the back of the truck. I'd have seen him when I was digging around for the tarp and stuff, but I didn't think to look along the road. He could have jumped off earlier and been picked up by the driver of the other car."

"Or he might be hurt," Megan said again.

"Guess it doesn't do much good to speculate. One thing's for sure, I need to let Agent Tucker know he didn't come back with you."

Passing the Sutherlands' road, Jennie noticed the lights were on but saw no vehicles in the driveway. Not surprising. Christine probably got word Aleshia had been arrested and went to the jail to bail her out or at least get a lawyer involved. That poor woman. Jennie sighed. The mink raid, losing her husband, her daughter getting arrested—an awful lot for one person to go through in a weekend. Which brought up another point. Maybe someone was targeting her. But why? Agent Tucker had mentioned Tom's offer to buy the farm. Much as she hated to admit it, the possibility existed that Tom was somehow involved.

"Megan, did you know Christine was putting her place up for sale?"

"No. Where did you hear that?"

"Agent Tucker. He said your dad was interested in buying it."

She shrugged. "That's news to me. I'm not surprised, though. Dad has talked about expanding."

Tom could have killed Sutherland. Now it looked as though

he had motive, means, and opportunity. He could have followed them into the mountains. Running Scott off the road, however, was another matter. *Speculation, McGrady. Sheer speculation.*

Sutherland's truck hit Scott. Of course, they had no real proof of that. Now with the truck mangled even more, they might never be able to prove it. There were too many pieces missing. Part of the problem may be that she kept trying to tie all the incidents together. ARM could be responsible for releasing the mink as they claimed. They may have been responsible for running her and Tucker off the road. Sal could have informed them of the arrest. Yes. That made sense. If she separated those out, it left Sutherland's murder and Scott's hit-and-run.

Jennie rubbed her forehead where a headache had started. "I need to quit thinking about this. It's making me crazy."

"Then don't think about it." Megan smiled. "You don't have to, you know. It's not your job."

Lisa chuckled. "She has a point, Jen. Maybe you need to back off on this one. Let the cops handle it. Our folks are coming out tomorrow for the barbecue. Then we go home. You don't have enough time. You can't win them all. Besides, you could get hurt." She sobered. "Or killed."

"You almost did tonight." Megan drove the point home. She groaned and pointed to the car making a left in front of them. "I was hoping we'd beat them home."

Tom and Mary pulled into the driveway just ahead of them. Jennie eyed the taillights. She didn't think they were a match, but what did she know? Her brain was pure mush.

"What are we going to tell my parents?" Megan asked. "They'll kill me if they find out what we did."

"Tell them the truth. It'll be better coming from us than the sheriff or Agent Tucker." Jennie pulled in beside the Bergstroms and braced herself for the fury that was bound to come their way.

Tom held the door for them, his nose wrinkling as Jennie ducked under his arm. "You kids have a bonfire tonight?"

"Not exactly." Jennie took her smoke-saturated jacket off and hung it over a chair on the porch to air out. "It's a long story. You and Mary might want to sit down. I'll fix us all some tea."

"Something tells me I'm not going to like this." Mary hung up her coat in the entry. Her concerned gaze settled on Jennie. "My goodness. You look terrible—what happened to you?"

"Like I said, it's a long story. Um—I need to make a phone call first, though." Jennie used the kitchen phone and called the sheriff's office. Tess answered.

Jennie told her about Sal not coming back with the others and relayed her suspicions. "I'm not sure how he managed it, but he may have been responsible for the ambush."

"Appreciate the call, Jennie. I'll get right on it."

"You'll let Agent Tucker know?"

"I will."

"Um—do you know what happened to Scott?"

"No, I'm afraid not." Tess wasn't offering any kind of information.

"What about Aleshia and Crystal?" she heard herself asking.

"They're here with Christine and their lawyer. I need to get back to them."

"Could you have Agent Tucker call me tomorrow?"

"I'll make a note of it." Tess sounded curt and annoyed. Though she didn't say it, Jennie sensed the stay-out-of-this tone in her voice. Not that she blamed the woman. By going out to meet Crystal, Jennie had caused more problems than she'd helped to resolve. Maybe she was losing her touch. Lisa was right. *You can't win them all.* Oh, but she wanted to.

Jennie joined the others around the dining room table. The teakettle whistled, and Mary brought it and a canister of tea to the table. Megan and Lisa had already told them about Crystal's brother agreeing to take Jennie to meet with his sister.

"I know we shouldn't have gone, but we wanted to find out what had happened to Scott." Megan picked out a raspberry tea bag and began dunking it. "Talking to Crystal seemed like a step in the right direction. We had no idea she was a member of ARM."

"I thought she might be," Jennie said. "This whole thing is my fault. I should have called Agent Tucker. I didn't because I knew he'd never let us go. That was my first mistake. My second was going with Crystal alone. All I could think about was finding Scott. I should have called the FBI as soon as I heard about Sal. As it turned out, I didn't have to. Tucker had a tail on Sal the whole time. Which turned out to be a good thing."

"And did you find Scott?" Tom asked.

"Yes." Jennie blew on her ginseng tea and took a sip. It went down smooth and warm. "Crystal and Aleshia helped him escape from the hospital. They thought he was with ARM. I don't think I was in any real danger from them—at least not right then. I'm not sure what would have happened if and when they found out the truth about Scott working for the FBI. And I'm sure they would have eventually." Jennie told them about the conversations she'd had and about the Sutherlands' truck being used to run Scott down. "I don't think it was Aleshia, but it had to be someone with access to the truck. Maybe Christine, Jim, or Stan . . ."

"Or me," Tom said.

Jennie did a double take.

Tom shook his head. "No, Jennie, I didn't do it. The point I was trying to make is that anyone could have taken that truck. Bob kept an extra set of keys in the shop."

"That's what makes this case so confusing. The one thing I do know is that neither Aleshia nor Crystal set fire to the road."

"Whoa." Tom held out his hand. "I think you'd better back up. How did you get from discussing politics with Aleshia to a fire?"

Jennie filled in the details. When she'd finished, Tom thoughtfully drank the last of his tea. They'd taken the news fairly well, Jennie thought. Much better than her own parents might have.

"Well." Tom set his cup down and stretched. Glancing at Mary, he said, "I think we'd all better get to bed, don't you?"

"That's a wonderful idea." She got to her feet and gathered the empty cups.

The girls looked at one another.

Megan pushed her chair back. "Aren't you going to yell at us and tell us we shouldn't have driven up there?"

"No. I figure Agent Tucker took care of that. The only thing I plan to do is not let you girls go anywhere else until you head for home." He held out his hand. "Jennie, your keys. Megan, you too."

Jennie handed them over without protest. Megan did so with an exaggerated groan. They were getting off easy. With the way she felt now, Jennie had no intention of going anywhere. The only thing she wanted to do was go home and forget—no, she wouldn't forget. She'd call Agent Tucker or Tess every day. Sometimes she hated being so tenacious. She didn't let go of things easily. That was one of the things she had in common with Gram and her father. None of them could walk away from an investigation. They had a propensity for justice that at times made them obsessive. *Hang it up, McGrady*, she told herself again. *Just walk away and leave the case to someone who knows what they're doing.*

Without another word, Tom locked the kitchen door and began turning off the lights. Jennie followed the girls upstairs and into the bedroom.

"I still can't see where we did anything all that wrong." Megan shut the door and flopped down on her bed.

"It's a hard call. At the time, I thought we were doing the right thing. Looking back, I see that it was a stupid idea to go. I put us all in danger. I should have just talked to Sal and convinced him to tell the Feds where Crystal was. It turned out okay, but what if the FBI hadn't shown up?"

"Jennie's right. Not about being to blame—we all made the choice to go. In fact, we talked you into it. Someone out there killed Mr. Sutherland and tried to kill Scott. Maybe they were trying to kill Jennie and Agent Tucker too. I vote we forget about it and try to enjoy the rest of the weekend. Maybe we can go swimming tomorrow or at least sit in the hot tub."

"The hot tub sounds so good." Jennie pulled her shirt over her head. "Do you think your folks would mind if we used the Jacuzzi tonight? I'm starting to feel really sore."

"Sounds good to me too. I'll ask."

While she was gone, Jennie finished undressing. "I need a shower."

"No kidding," Lisa said with a smile. "Go ahead. We'll wait for you."

When Jennie got out of the shower, Lisa and Megan had their suits on. "Dad said yes. We just need to be quiet, and we can't stay out there for more than half an hour."

"You guys go ahead. I'll get my suit on and be right there."

Several minutes later, Jennie stuffed her smoke-tainted clothes into a plastic bag and dropped them into the laundry room on her way out. Tomorrow she'd wash them.

Megan and Lisa had just gotten the lid off the hot tub and were getting in when Jennie joined them. "Turn off the porch light so we can see the stars," Megan said.

Jennie did. A full yellow harvest moon provided more than enough light, and the darkness magnified the brightness of the stars. The 104-degree water felt hot going in, but Jennie adjusted to it quickly. The pulsing jets and heat soothed her frazzled nerves and nearly put her to sleep. Lisa and Megan began talking about Kyle and Algie. Jennie didn't feel much like conversing, so she leaned back, looked up at the stars, and thought about Ryan. He loved nights like this. They would often sit out on their rocks overlooking the ocean and talk about life. Was he sitting there with Camilla now? Were they talking about God and solving the world's problems? Tears gathered in her eyes. She lifted her hands to her face and washed them away. Jennie didn't hate him anymore—she never really had. He was right, of course. They were still friends. She missed him and vowed that as soon as she got home, she'd call him and tell him. If he wanted to date Camilla, he should. Just like she should figure out how she really felt about Scott. Was it just physical attraction or something deeper? She missed him, too, and made a mental note to talk to Agent Tucker. If he wouldn't disclose Scott's whereabouts, maybe he could get a message to him.

By the time they trudged back up to the bedroom, she felt like a mass of pliable clay. She fell asleep before the lights went out.

———

Jennie awoke with a start at six A.M. She'd slept soundly and hadn't even dreamed—at least not that she could remember. She stretched and wished she hadn't. Every muscle in her body hurt. Jennie found a comfortable position on her stomach and debated between staying in bed and getting up.

Lying there in the stillness of the morning, she waited for her brain to kick in. She thought about what Megan had said the night before. *"It's not your job, Jennie."* So true. She wasn't a detective yet and might never be one. Still, she wanted so badly for the killer to be caught. *Don't let whoever did this get away, God*, she prayed silently. Gazing out the windows, she added, *And keep Scott safe*.

So far her resolve to mind her own business still remained strong, but then, she hadn't gotten out of bed yet. Jennie looked over at Megan, still sleeping and looking like a sweet cherub with riotous curls framing her face. On the bunk below, Lisa had a similar angelic expression. Jennie smiled, wondering if she looked that innocent and attractive while she slept. Probably not.

Climbing down from the top bunk, she padded to the dresser, turned on a small lamp, and looked in the mirror. Squinting at her reflection, she muttered, "Definitely not." Her hair was a matted mess from having gone to bed with it wet. She dug a brush out of her bag and, going to the window, brushed out the snarls. The sun was just rising, coloring the fluffy clouds on the horizon in a rosy hue. It would be light soon. In the room next door she heard water running. Tom would be getting ready to go out to the barns.

Jim's car sat in front of the other house. Lights were on in the living room. He would be getting ready for work as well. She frowned. Was he out on bail, or had he been released for lack of evidence? How long had he been out? As early as yesterday? Early enough to head for the mountains and rendezvous with Aleshia?

She went back to the dresser and turned out the light so she could watch without being seen. Last night she'd come to terms with not trying to solve the case, but now, looking at Jim's car, she was having second thoughts. While it didn't bother her to back off, it did bother her to know that Bob Sutherland's killer was still out there—and that it could be Jim Owens.

There was one way to find out. Jennie tightened her hold on the brush and hurriedly finished her hair. She secured it at the nape of her neck with a scrunchie, then pulled on a fresh pair of jeans, a turtleneck, and a sweat shirt.

So much for staying out of the investigation, a sarcastic voice in her head seemed to say. *I am*, she thought back. *I'm just going to help with the chores. While I'm at it, I might look at the taillights on Jim's car. And maybe find out when he was released.*

22

"You're up early this morning." Tom walked into the kitchen as Jennie was buttering a slice of toast.

"Yeah. I was awake, so I thought I'd help with the chores."

"Trying to make up for last night?" His teasing smile told her he was no longer angry.

"Maybe," she teased back. "But look at it this way. If I'm working with you, I can't get into any more trouble."

"You have a point." He pulled a stained one-piece orange coverall off a hook and began pulling it on over his jeans.

"Would you like me to fix you something to eat?" Jennie put the margarine away and ambled to the porch.

"No, thanks." He pulled the suit up, maneuvered his arms into it, zipped himself in, and reached for his boots.

Holding the toast in her mouth, Jennie looked for and found the boots she'd worn before and slipped them onto her stockinged feet. Brushing the crumbs from her hands, she said, "I notice Jim's car is here. He must be out of jail, huh?"

"Yep."

"When did they let him go?"

"Yesterday, around dinnertime. He called just before Mary and I left for Salem."

"Guess you're glad about that. I mean, with him being your hired hand and all."

"I am relieved. Said all along he couldn't have done it."

Jennie still wasn't convinced of that. He could have had an accomplice—like Aleshia. "I hope they find out who did."

166

"So do I, Jennie." He pulled open the door and waited for her to step outside. "So do I."

As they walked behind Jim's car, Jennie imagined the car she'd seen on the mountain. The taillights were about the right distance apart and rectangular. The car was a dark maroon. He could have done it, but she didn't think he would have been able to follow them. The timing was wrong for that—just like it was for Mr. Sutherland's murder. Still, he could be involved. He could even have hired someone to do it.

Maybe he is secretly involved with ARM and was going to meet Aleshia. He could, as she'd thought before, be Sonja. What better cover than to work on a fur farm? Agent Tucker had said the word was out on the Internet about Scott's involvement with the FBI. Had he gotten that information and gone to warn Aleshia and Crystal?

Jim opened the door, scattering Jennie's thoughts.

"Mornin', Tom, Jennie." He bounded down the stairs and fell into step beside Jennie.

"Morning." Tom nodded. "Glad to see you made it back."

"Confessing like that was a pretty stupid thing to do. I was just afraid Aleshia might have done it. She didn't, of course," he said quickly.

"How can you be so sure?" Jennie asked.

"For one thing, like Christine said, Aleshia wouldn't have put Sasha's carcass in the freezer or the trash. She wouldn't have touched it. If she did anything, it would have been to bury it."

Jennie started at the idea. He had a point.

Jim nodded toward her. "Heard you had an interesting night last night."

Jennie shrugged. "Word gets around fast. How did you find out?"

"I was at the sheriff's office when the call came in about the accident."

"Accident?"

"Um—yeah. We didn't get many details, just that there was an accident involving you and that FBI agent."

"It was definitely not an accident, Jim," Tom said. "At least not to hear Jennie tell it. Someone ambushed them—poured gas all over the road and tossed a Molotov cocktail into it. Then tossed another at the truck. Tucker swerved to avoid it. Strange business," Tom added. "Sounds to me like something ARM might do."

"Could be," Jim said. "More'n likely, though, someone is trying to make it look like ARM is responsible. ARM doesn't—or hasn't before—attacked individuals. When they do hit, it's usually to make a statement or to release animals. They've always taken credit for their acts."

"What about the fire bombs and damage they do to places that serve meat?" Jennie asked.

"They make sure there are no people around." Jim paused to open the shop door.

"That's not entirely true anymore. Remember the raid just west of here?" Tom reminded him about the hit made a few days before. "According to the memo from the Fur Commission, armed terrorists stormed the place and left the owner's son for dead. What's with you, Jim? Sounds like you're defending them."

"You know better than that. I'm just not convinced that ARM is responsible for everything that's been going on out here. I'll admit they seem to be getting more violent, but to murder somebody in cold blood?" Jim frowned. "I don't know. Aleshia still insists ARM had nothing to do with her dad's murder or with the hit-and-run. I tend to believe her."

"So you're saying ARM instigated the raids but nothing else?" Jennie asked.

Jim nodded. "That's my opinion."

"You might be right," Tom acquiesced. "If that's the case, one of our own might be a killer, and I hate to think that might be possible."

Jim shrugged. "It happens. Just because it isn't ARM doesn't mean the person who killed him was a local. Could have been a random act of violence. It also could have been one of the Hispanic gang members he's been spouting off about lately. He wasn't quiet about that, I can tell you."

Tom admitted that might be the case. "Bob has made his share of enemies."

Jim agreed. "There was that kid he fired just a day or two after he hired him—Sal something or other."

"Sal Chavez? Crystal's brother?" Tom asked.

"Yeah. The kid was looking for a part-time job. Christine hired him. Bob wasn't excited about the idea, but he agreed to take Sal on. I'm not sure whether Bob fired him because he's Mexican or because he wasn't doing his job. Either way, the kid couldn't have been too happy about it."

Jennie digested that last bit of information. She wondered if Tess or Agent Tucker knew about the gang business or Sal's being fired. Curious—Sal being Crystal's brother and all. Had he applied for the job so he could scope the place out? Or had he gotten the job because Crystal was Aleshia's friend? Could Sal have been seeking revenge? Somehow murder didn't fit the smiling face and the carefree attitude that Sal seemed to have.

Talk about whether or not ARM would resort to murder stopped as they set about doing the morning chores. Jennie received instructions from Jim and spent the next hour feeding the mink. The entire time, she wavered back and forth about who might have killed Mr. Sutherland and why. Was Jim the killer? Had he instigated it? Were he and Aleshia working together? Maybe they were working with Sal and Crystal. *Maybe you should forget it, McGrady. Admit you're not getting anywhere and let the police handle it.* Setting her questions aside, she decided she would call the sheriff and let her know what Jim had said about Sal.

When she'd finished, Jennie put the tractor away and found Jim and Tom in the shop skinning pelts. At least a dozen dead animals lay in a heap at one end of the counter. Jennie's stomach rolled. She focused on the concrete under her feet. She would never be able to handle that kind of work. Both men, however, acted as though skinning the animals was as normal a task as brushing their teeth. For them it was.

If Aleshia was so against fur farming, Jennie again wondered how she could stand to be engaged to a man who killed the animals she loved for a living. It didn't make a lot of sense.

"If you don't mind," Jim said, "I'd like to go over to the Sutherlands' for a few minutes when we're done here to see how Aleshia and Christine are doing. This whole thing has been rough on both of them."

"Sure, no problem." Tom grabbed another mink. "You can take the rest of the day off if you want. We have guests coming. Won't need you until tomorrow morning."

"Thanks. I'm hoping I can talk Aleshia into getting out of ARM. It's a good time. She didn't much like being arrested. She's starting to get disillusioned, what with the increasing violence and the raid on her parents' place."

"Well, I wouldn't hold my breath. Amazes me that you two are still together." Tom shrugged. "To each his own, I suppose."

Jim chuckled. "It gets interesting at times, and we have some pretty hot debates. Thing is, I love her, Tom. And she loves me. We don't have to agree on everything."

"That's true enough. Mary and I disagree on a number of issues. Still, if she became a member of ARM, I'm not sure I could handle that."

"Well, it's a little different for you and Mary. You own the ranch. I don't plan on staying in the business that much longer. Been thinking of going back to school and getting a degree in engineering."

"Yeah?" Tom nodded. "That's not a bad field."

"Excuse me," Jennie cut in. "I'm finished with the feeding. Um—I think I'll go back up to the house."

"Okay. Thanks for the help." Tom waved at her. "See you in a while."

Tom and Jim went back to their conversation, and Jennie jogged back to the house.

"Good morning, Jennie," Mary greeted her in a cheerful voice. "Don't tell me you've been out working already."

"Okay, I won't." Jennie kicked her boots off and went in to wash her hands.

Mary laughed. "Are you hungry? I have some oatmeal baking and I just finished cooking up some bacon."

"Mmm. I love baked oatmeal. But I think I'd like to shower first."

"Take your time. It won't be ready for another twenty minutes."

Jennie tiptoed around the bedroom so she wouldn't arouse the sleeping beauties. In a way, she wished she were still sleeping, but there'd be little point in going to bed. She was too keyed up to sleep. Instead, she showered, dressed, braided her hair, then gathered up her dirty laundry and headed downstairs. Mary showed her how to use the washer, and a few minutes later she had a load agitating.

It was only eight, but Jennie felt like she'd been up for hours. When she returned to the kitchen, Mary had two places set on the table. "Looks like it will be just you and me for now. The girls may be asleep for a while—Megan likes to sleep late. Tom wants to finish the order before he eats."

Jennie pulled out a chair. "Fine with me. I'd like to talk to you anyway."

"Oh?" She sat down. "About anything special?"

Jennie scooped a generous portion of oatmeal out of the baking dish, then reached for the milk. "Agent Tucker said Christine is selling her farm. I was curious about that. I mean—they haven't even had Mr. Sutherland's funeral yet. He also said Tom might buy it."

"Yes, Tom and I talked about it. If she does sell, we'd like first option." Mary secured a piece of bacon and waved it in the air while she talked. "I'm hoping she'll back off and wait for a while, though. Hate to see anyone make such important decisions during a crisis. I think she's afraid she won't be able to take care of it, but like I told her, she has Stan. Jim can help—Tom, too, if it comes to that."

Jennie sprinkled on cinnamon and took a bite. "Had you thought about buying it before?"

"Christine mentioned that they might sell a year or so ago. She'd been after Bob to retire. Tom said then he'd be interested, but they never brought it up again. Which is fine." She poured a glass of orange juice and offered the pitcher to Jennie. "I wish Tom hadn't been so quick to offer this time. Agent Tucker practically accused him of murdering Bob for the land—which is insane. He has been wanting to expand, and having the barns already set up would be a bonus—price is right, too, but we certainly wouldn't kill for it."

Jennie nodded, glad Mary had brought up the investigation. "Tucker is looking for motive."

"I suppose they need to look at all the possibilities, but I can't help but be offended. Tom wouldn't hurt anyone."

"Do you know Sal—Algie's friend?"

"Not well. He's been here swimming a few times."

Jennie told her about Sal's short-lived job at the Sutherlands' and her suspicions about him being connected with the murder and the attempt on Scott's life. "He may have been the one responsible for the explosion last night."

"I hope not, Jennie. I'd hate to think any of Megan's friends would be involved in anything so violent."

"Yeah. Well, I need to tell Sheriff Parker about the job. They may already know, but it could be an important clue."

"Mmm." The buzzer on the stove went off, and Mary jumped up. She turned it off and pulled out a second pan of baked oatmeal. From the counter she took two casserole dishes covered in aluminum foil and set them in the oven.

"Isn't that a lot of oatmeal?"

"I always make extra and freeze it. The casseroles are for dinner tonight—one of them is. The other I'll be sending over to Christine. I invited her to join us for dinner, but she's not up to company. I'm concerned about her. She's withdrawing, but that's understandable with all she's been through. I just wish this business would end and the police would find the killer."

"Me too." Jennie savored the salty, crunchy texture of the bacon. They ate in companionable silence for several minutes.

"This has been quite a visit, hasn't it?" Mary gave her a dimpled smile and sipped at her coffee.

"No kidding. I had a feeling something would happen, but I sure didn't expect all this."

The phone rang. Mary jumped up to get it, and after a brief conversation pointed the phone to Jennie. "Agent Tucker wants to talk to you."

Coming to the phone, Jennie felt oddly nervous. "Hello?"

"How's it going, Jennie?" he asked, apparently not expecting an answer. "Tess said you wanted me to call."

"I did. I wondered how you were."

"Other than feeling like I've been run down by a semi, great." He sounded annoyed. Jennie didn't blame him.

"Um—I was hoping you could tell me what happened to Scott."

"No can do, Jennie. I'm not even sure myself. We took him to Portland, and the supervisor up there was taking care of him."

"Is there any chance they'll let me see him?"

"I don't see why not. Call the office when you get back home."

"There's something else." Jennie told him about Sal's short-term employment with the Sutherlands.

"Thanks for the info. I'll check into it. Hmm. Wonder why Christine didn't give me his name when I asked for possible suspects? 'Course, she was pretty upset."

"Well, he is Crystal's brother and—maybe she didn't want him to get into trouble." Jennie twisted the cord around her finger. "Which reminds me, did you find him?"

"Not yet, but we will."

"I heard you let Aleshia and Crystal go."

"Yep. Not enough to hold them. Scott wasn't able to get much information—nothing on Sonja, which was why he went with them in the first place. Can't bring charges against them for printing propaganda."

"Jim says he's going to try to talk Aleshia into getting out of ARM."

He laughed at that. "More power to him. Look, I have to go. Sheriff Parker just came in."

Jennie hung up, wishing she were staying on—wishing she were an adult so she could officially work on investigations. *What would you do then, McGrady?* she asked herself.

Write it all out, she answered, *and put the pieces together.* She was missing something important. Okay, maybe she'd never figure it out, but she had to try.

Jennie finished eating and excused herself to go upstairs. Lisa and Megan were still asleep. She was ready to scream—not at them—it didn't really bother her that they were sleeping in. What bothered her was this stupid case. Why couldn't she figure it out? If ARM hadn't killed Sutherland, who had? Had the same person committed all the crimes?

Jennie made her chart, listing the suspects along one side of the paper. Then on the top of the page she wrote *motive, means,* and *opportunity*. Drawing a line under each person involved, she made a note under each heading. Her suspects included Tom, Mary, Christine, Aleshia, Jim, Crystal, and Sal.

She began the process of elimination based on the premise that Scott's hit-and-run, Sutherland's murder, and the attempt on hers and Tucker's life had been done by the same person. Since Tom and Mary were at home and couldn't have run Scott down, Jennie crossed them off the list. Christine was in town shopping when Sutherland had been killed. Aleshia said she'd seen her dad after her mom left. Jennie put a line through Christine's name as well.

Aleshia, Crystal, and Jim couldn't have been responsible for the accident on the mountain. Sal could have been around for all of them. But somehow Jennie didn't think he was the one. Again she came back to the possibility that the incidents maybe weren't connected. Either that, or someone was lying, which was entirely possible. Then again, maybe she hadn't yet written the killer's name down.

Mr. Sutherland had told Scott he knew who Sonja was. She added Sonja to the list. Maybe ARM wasn't taking responsibility for anything but the raids, but that didn't mean Sonja or another ARM member hadn't done it.

Sal seemed to be a key figure in all of this. Jennie wanted to drive over to Crystal's and find out if Sal, too, was involved with ARM. Unfortunately, Tom had her keys. She took her note pad and pen and headed downstairs. Maybe she couldn't drive over, but she could call. While she still had a hard time casting Sal in the role of a killer, she sensed he was deeply involved. Her intuition painted him more as a victim. Either way, he was in mighty big trouble, and Jennie felt compelled to dig deeper.

23

Settling into an overstuffed chair, Jennie paged through the phone book. When she'd found the number, she dialed Crystal. The nurse answered on the first ring.

"Crystal, this is Jennie McGrady."

"Oh." The tone of her voice clearly indicated disapproval. "What do you want?"

"I was wondering if you'd heard from Sal."

"No. And I blame you for this. If you hadn't talked him into bringing you—"

"Hey, I wasn't the one who took a patient out of the hospital and hid him in the woods."

There was a long silence. For a moment Jennie thought she'd hung up. "I'm sorry. You're right. I have no one to blame but myself. I never should have become involved with ARM." Her voice broke. "I'll never forgive myself if my actions have caused danger to my brother. He's a good boy, Jennie."

"Is he a member of ARM?"

"No. He's much too young."

Jennie didn't think so but didn't comment.

"I heard he worked for the Sutherlands for a short time."

"Yes." She sounded wary.

"And Mr. Sutherland fired him?"

"Yes—why are you asking?"

Jennie doodled on the paper while she talked. "Do you know why he was fired?"

"It didn't work out."

"Did he get along all right with Mr. Sutherland?"

"I don't know. He's a very demanding boss, and Sal doesn't like too much pressure."

"Why did he take the job in the first place?"

"He needed something part time. I mentioned it to Aleshia. She told her mother, and Christine said they could use someone through the pelting season."

"Was Sal angry about being let go?"

"Not really. Sal's an easygoing guy. If you're thinking he killed Mr. Sutherland, you can forget it. But I'm really concerned. It's not like Sal to stay away. He knows how Mama and I worry about him. If he were able, he'd at least call. I'm so afraid for him, Jennie."

Jennie told Crystal about Jim's plan to talk to Aleshia about leaving ARM. "Maybe you both should leave. There's another organization—an animal protection group that seems a lot more practical."

"Yes, Scott mentioned that last night. I may, but I doubt Aleshia would. She's very dedicated."

"But you're not?"

"I came close to losing my job—fortunately, Scott didn't disclose my involvement in getting him out of the hospital. He took full responsibility for checking himself out against doctor's orders."

They spoke for several more minutes before Jennie rang off. Her suspicions about Sal had given way to concern for his safety.

Mary peeked into the living room. "Oh good, you're off the phone. I need to call Christine. Did I hear you mention Sal?"

"Yes. I was talking to Crystal. She hasn't heard from him."

"That's too bad. I certainly hope they find him and that he hasn't come to any harm."

"Agent Tucker said they were still looking for him." Jennie frowned. "At least now I'm pretty sure he isn't one of the bad guys."

"Oh? What makes you say that?"

"Something Crystal said. Apparently Sal is in the habit of checking in every so often. Doesn't like to worry his mother. Crystal said he'd have called her or at least gotten word that he was okay. The fact that he hasn't checked in makes me wonder if he's been injured or worse." Jennie stood. "The phone's all yours."

Mary thanked her, dialed, and waited.

"Oh, hi, Christine—I thought maybe you'd gone. I didn't wake you, did I?"

Jennie didn't mean to eavesdrop and had gone back into the living room, but Mary's voice carried.

"I baked a chicken and wild rice casserole for you and Aleshia for dinner tonight," Mary said.

Jennie watched out the front window as Jim emerged from the house and got into the car, backed around, and drove out. She concentrated on the taillights when he braked. It wasn't his car that she'd seen the night before. The taillights were too long and narrow. The car she'd seen was smaller and the taillights more rounded.

After a long pause, Mary said, "Nonsense—it's no trouble at all. I can have Jim bring it over." Another pause. "Yes, he's concerned about you. I suspect he'll be over soon."

Jennie hurried into the kitchen to tell Mary that Jim had already left.

Mary hung up the phone. "Is something wrong?"

"Just that Jim just took off."

"Well, no matter. I'll run it over there myself."

"I'll do it. I need something to do anyway."

"Thanks, Jennie. That would be a big help. I'll call Christine and let her know you're coming."

Jennie slipped on her tennis shoes while Mary settled the hot dish in a basket with a loaf of bread, a bottle of sparkling cider, a package of premixed salad, and some fruit. Jennie felt a little like Red Riding Hood carrying the basket. She took the lake trail and once again experienced a sense of unease at being alone. She'd tried to get Drooley to come along, but he had declined, choosing instead to lie in the warm kitchen with his small patient and the comforting scents of the dinner to come.

When she arrived at the Sutherlands', Jennie thought at first no one was there. The driveway was empty. It seemed strange they'd all be gone. Hadn't Jim said he was coming here? Jennie went up to the door and rang the bell. If nothing else, she could leave the basket on the front porch.

On the second buzz, Christine opened the door. Jennie suspected she'd interrupted her as she was getting dressed. She was wearing jeans rather than her usual dress, and a plaid tuck-in shirt with the sleeves folded to her elbows. She had no shoes or socks and wore no makeup. Not that makeup would have done much good. Christine looked like she'd been crying. "Hi, Jennie. Thanks for bringing it over. I told Mary she didn't have to do all this."

Jennie smiled. "That's the way she is."

"Yes, a regular Martha Stewart." Jennie didn't miss the sarcasm in Christine's voice. That seemed odd. Christine had a similar propensity for doing for others and showed it when she invited Jennie in for tea. Of course, Jennie didn't blame the woman for feeling out of sorts.

She nodded toward the driveway. "I didn't think anyone was home."

"My car is in the garage."

Jennie was disappointed. Part of her reason for coming over was to get a look at Aleshia's and Christine's cars. She also wanted to talk to Aleshia about Sal.

"What about Aleshia and Jim? I thought Jim was coming over here."

"He was but decided to meet Aleshia in town. She's gone in to be with Crystal." Christine shook her head. "It never seems to end, does it? I certainly hope no harm comes to the boy. He was taking a chance staying in the woods alone like that. Asking for trouble."

Jennie shifted the basket to her left hand. "It's kind of heavy. Where would you like me to put this?"

"I'll take it." She surprised Jennie by effortlessly snatching it up and setting it on the counter. "Have a seat—I'll get you some tea. Is that all right, or would you rather have hot chocolate?"

"Tea is fine."

Christine poured hot water into two cups and set them on the table. "I'm glad you came, Jennie. I was hoping for an opportunity to talk with you. Have you had breakfast?"

"Yes."

She reached into the refrigerator and brought out a carton of eggs, then filled a pan with water, settling all twelve eggs into it.

"You're eating all those?"

Christine smiled. "I'm making egg salad for sandwiches later."

"Oh." Jennie felt embarrassed for asking. "What did you want to talk to me about?"

"I understand you're quite the little detective."

Jennie couldn't tell if she was being sincere or sarcastic. "Where did you hear that?"

"Aleshia said you'd managed to track down your friend and lead the FBI to them. They weren't doing anything wrong, you know."

"Weren't they? I know it isn't a crime to belong to ARM, but it seems to me she's playing with fire."

Christine gave her an odd look and returned to the table. "She's careful."

"How much did Aleshia tell you about their trip into the mountains?"

"Not much. I didn't realize she'd gone with Crystal until after I got back home that morning I saw you at Crystal's. When I got home, there was a message on my answering machine."

"Did you know they'd taken Scott?" Jennie asked.

"Not until you told me he'd disappeared from the hospital. I put two and two together and realized he was probably with them."

"Did you know someone tried to blow Agent Tucker and me off the road?"

"I heard. Must have been frightening for you."

"It was. Considering the way it was done, I have a hunch whoever did it was with ARM. Maybe they were retaliating because of Crystal's and Aleshia's arrest. In fact, I think that one person is responsible for everything that's been happening."

"Do you have any idea who that is?"

"Maybe Sal—Crystal's brother. I keep going back and forth about him. He did know where the girls were camped, and he stayed up in the woods. Maybe he met somebody else up there— or maybe he was working alone."

"Do you think he might be a member of ARM?"

"It's possible."

"From what Aleshia tells me about ARM, Jennie, you're wrong. Their agenda doesn't include murder or attacks on individuals."

Jennie sipped on the too-hot tea. "I was hoping I could talk to Aleshia about Sal. I know the pieces will fall together eventually. I saw the taillights of the car the person who ambushed us was driving. Can't remember that much about it yet. It'll come back eventually."

"Maybe you should hope it doesn't. My husband died because he got too close to the truth. I wouldn't want the same thing to happen to you."

For the next few moments neither spoke. The stove fan whirred and the clock above the sink ticked. Jennie couldn't pinpoint exactly what had triggered it for her, but crazy as it seemed, her suspicions pointed to Christine as the killer. The last comment, though wrapped in concern, held the hard edge of a threat. Her mind replayed the inconsistencies. Christine's strength as she lifted the heavy basket with practiced ease. The car in the garage. Maybe Aleshia, like Jennie, had thought no one was at home the day Mr. Sutherland had been killed, but Christine could have been there the whole time. She could have lied about when she left for town. How would Christine react to her husband if she knew what he'd done to Aleshia's fox?

Jennie imagined the scene. Aleshia comes, fights with her father, runs into Jim, then leaves. Christine may not have even known she was there. She gets ready to go into town, then goes out to say good-bye to her husband. He tells her about Aleshia pushing him. Maybe he's struggling to get up. Christine sees what he's done with Sasha and grabs the hammer. If she was home when Aleshia left, she would have had plenty of time to kill him, dispose of the evidence, and drive into town to meet Aleshia at the restaurant.

But that couldn't have been the only motive. *Wait.* Scott said Sutherland was close to finding out who Sonja was. Could he have confronted her? Could he have discovered that his own wife was not only a member of ARM, but the leader—that she'd turned their daughter against him? Christine seemed almost proud of

Aleshia's affiliation with the radical protest group. Something else. Christine had easy access to the truck. She could have run Scott off the road. She could have been the person on the mountain.

No. Jennie reeled in her imagination. The idea was too far-fetched.

Christine couldn't be Sonja. The ARM leader traveled around the country. Christine had been living here since Aleshia was in grade school. There was no logic to her sudden suspicion, but Jennie couldn't let it go. She needed proof one way or the other. Maybe if she could see Christine's car . . .

Jennie glanced at the long hallway. The house was a split level with the main part of the house at ground level and the basement and possibly other rooms below. Jennie had gotten familiar with the layout—outside, at least, while they'd been picking up the released mink. She had an idea.

"Um—do you mind if I use your bathroom? Tea tends to run right through me."

Christine pulled back from wherever her thoughts had taken her. "Sure. It's down the hall—second door on the right—across from the stairs."

Stairs. Yes. Those stairs would lead to the garage—Jennie was sure of it. She'd run the fan in the bathroom, then slip out, check the taillights on the car, and leave through the garage. If Christine was guilty, Jennie would hurry back to Bergstroms' and call the sheriff. If she found nothing, she'd go back upstairs and finish her tea, then leave. Maybe she'd tell Tess or the FBI agent about her suspicions—maybe not.

Christine left the table and opened the basket Mary had prepared. With any luck, she'd be busy with her breakfast and kitchen things. Jennie hurried into the bathroom and turned on the fan, then slipped out, looking down the hall toward the kitchen to make certain Christine wasn't watching. She dashed across the hall and down the stairs. There were three doors. The one to her left was a laundry room, the one straight in front stood open and looked like a craft room. Jennie started to turn right, but the faint scent of gasoline stopped her. It drew her like a beacon into the laundry room. Jennie spotted a black turtleneck and stirrup pants, heavy socks, a ski mask, and knit gloves in a clump on the floor.

She picked up the gloves, brought them to her nose, and sniffed.

Part of her wanted to believe it was a coincidence and that Christine had gotten gas on her hands some other way than sloshing it all over the road just before Jennie and Agent Tucker came around the bend. Part of her felt the thrill of being one step closer to discovering the truth. Jennie glanced around for a plastic bag in which to store the gloves. When she didn't find one, she stashed them in a cupboard behind some rags where they'd be missed when Christine did her laundry.

Jennie's heart shifted into high gear as she stepped back into the hall and reached for the door leading into the garage. She needed to hurry so Christine wouldn't get suspicious. She'd look at the car on the way out, then go back to Bergstroms' and tell the sheriff what she'd found.

She remembered now. Christine's car was dark purple. Circling the car, she looked closely at the taillights. Rounded, like the ones that had passed them on the road and driven off, leaving her and Tucker to die.

As quietly as she could, Jennie began to pull open the garage door. She heard a click behind her, and the hum of a garage door opener. The wide door slammed back down, nearly jerking her arm out of the socket. She was trapped.

24

"Did you get lost, Jennie? The bathroom is upstairs." Christine stood in the doorway, the garage door opener pointed like a weapon.

Jennie gulped. "I . . . I know." She smiled. "You have a beautiful house. I couldn't resist looking around."

"Really. In that case, maybe you'd like to see more."

"N-no, I really need to get back to the Bergstroms'. Lisa and Megan will be waiting."

"Oh, Jennie." She looked genuinely distressed. "You really can't believe I'd let you leave now."

"I'm afraid I don't know what you mean." Jennie feigned innocence.

"Don't you? You're a smart girl. I could tell you were going to be trouble from the start. You're too inquisitive. And that boyfriend of yours . . ." She shook her head. "I knew something was fishy when he told me about Melissa. I didn't realize it at the time, but Scott's testimony put Melissa in prison, and the FBI used her computer and code name to e-mail me about him. It didn't sound quite like her, so I contacted her partner. Paul told me all about Scott and how he wanted to get even with ARM for that fireman's death. Scott is a fool. Those deaths were accidental. We don't want to see people get hurt. The fire bombs we'd placed in the lab were supposed to set off the sprinkler system—not start a major fire. It wasn't our fault their sprinklers failed."

"Right." Jennie reached behind her and felt for the handle. "And I suppose it was Mr. Sutherland's fault that you killed him."

"In a way, yes. He was getting out of control. He threatened to go to the police and tell them that Aleshia was Sonja. I couldn't let that happen."

"Aleshia? But you—"

"Yes, Jennie. I am Sonja. Not even my husband would have guessed it was me. Unfortunately, if he'd gone to the FBI with what he knew, they would have eventually figured it out. I didn't want to kill him." Christine's gaze dropped for a moment, reflecting her grief. "Funny thing—I did love him. I don't suppose anyone will believe that now."

"Probably not. Why did you go after Scott?"

"He was a traitor, and I wasn't certain how much he knew."

"How many more people will you have to kill, Christine? Me? Sal? What about Aleshia and Crystal? Do they know who you are?"

"Not yet. I'll have to tell Aleshia now that I've decided to leave here."

"Are you planning to kill them to protect your identity?"

Christine gave her a disgusted look. "That won't be necessary. You forget they are loyal to ARM. Aleshia will be thrilled to be allowed into the inner circle."

"Why didn't you tell Aleshia before?" Jennie reached behind her and gripped the door handle. Maybe she could distract Christine long enough to jerk up the door and dive under it.

"It was best she not know." Christine leaned against her car.

"What happens when she finds out you killed her father?"

"She won't."

"How did you know where to find them?"

"You're just full of questions, aren't you?"

Jennie shrugged. "I'm curious. Since you don't plan on letting me go and I already know you're the killer, why not indulge me?"

"Why not? It's all rather complicated. I thought I had dealt with your Mr. Chambers. I should have stopped to make certain he was dead. Big mistake. By the time I realized he hadn't died, it was too late to warn Aleshia. I had to find them before the FBI did. I didn't know exactly where they were, so I called Crystal's mother. She didn't know either. Sal told me the general area but wouldn't give me any details. He said he'd give them a message for me, so I knew he planned to go up there. I waited—an interesting scenario. As I suspected, the FBI was waiting too. I followed you all into the mountains. My plan was to warn them about Scott and get them out of there. Unfortunately I didn't arrive soon enough."

"Why did you sabotage Tucker and me?"

"Several reasons. You were Scott's friend. I didn't know how much he'd told you." She sighed deeply. "And you seem to have trouble minding your own business. Besides that, I saw a chance to get rid of another FBI agent. I don't know which of you was most dangerous. Learning that Melissa had been arrested concerned me. They were getting too close."

Jennie lifted up on the garage door. It wouldn't budge. Frightened didn't begin to explain Jennie's feelings. She was trapped in a garage with a cold-blooded killer."

"It's locked," Christine said, looking at Jennie again. "And it will stay locked."

"Then I guess I'll hang around for a while." Jennie tried for a light tone but couldn't quite pull it off. *It'll be okay*, she reassured herself. Sooner or later she would catch Christine with her guard down and make a break for it. If not through the garage, then through the house. She needed to stay calm and in control. She'd look for an opportunity and take it. Jennie had no doubt she'd be faster and stronger than the gaunt, middle-aged woman. Christine wasn't carrying a gun—at least not yet. That gave Jennie a definite edge.

Christine signaled her to go back into the house. When Jennie started up the stairs, Christine grabbed her wrist and with surprising strength yanked her back down. "Not that way. Since you're so curious, I thought I'd show you how I managed to keep my identity secret for all these years."

"Sure." Jennie massaged her right wrist and swallowed back a wave of fear. She'd underestimated her adversary. Christine might be scrawny, but she was a lot stronger than Jennie had thought. She remembered then about ARM members being trained in martial arts. If that was true of Christine, escaping might not be an option. She'd play along for now. *Right, like you've got a choice.*

"Don't even think about leaving." Christine fastened her gaze on Jennie. "I have ways of making sure you won't."

"I don't doubt that for a minute," Jennie muttered.

"In there." She nodded toward the room Jennie thought was a craft room. Cabinets lined one wall. A sewing machine stood against a painted concrete wall beneath a high, curtained window. A bolt of fabric and miscellaneous sewing supplies were strewn on a craft table in the center of the room. Another wall was practically all closet. Christine slid open the doors.

What happened next looked like something out of a spy movie. Jennie watched mesmerized as Christine, alias Sonja, moved aside a few hangers and pressed a button on the back wall. It opened to reveal another room about fifteen by twenty. In it were two computers and work stations, file cabinets, and a table spread with maps. On a far wall was a large map with colored pins marking locations of what were probably hits by ARM members. But much more frightening was the weapons arsenal. An open cabinet displayed everything from assault rifles to hand grenades along with equipment needed to make bombs. Jennie recognized some of the paraphernalia from the article she'd seen on making fire bombs.

"This is my command center. I keep an eye on all ARM activities. As you can see, we've accomplished a great deal." She pointed to the map.

"Wow! I'm impressed. How did you do all this without your husband finding out? This must have been a huge job."

"Not really. I managed to stay involved on a superficial level until about ten years ago when we had this house built. It had been my dream to have a room like this, so I had the builders leave me the space as a finished storage area. Bob left the house—the design, everything—to me. He was too busy with his own affairs. There are some benefits in having a husband who's self-involved."

"I don't understand. If you hate the fur industry, how could you live here on the farm?"

"It hasn't been easy. For the most part I stayed away from the barns except to feed and care for the mink on occasion. I closed my eyes to what he and the Bergstroms were doing. Every day I would tell myself it was the best way to help the cause."

"How noble." Jennie felt sick. "I suppose you instigated the raid on your farm."

She smiled. "Oh yes. My moment of glory. I can't tell you how good it felt to finally be able to free those animals. Like an absolution."

"Excuse me if I don't share your enthusiasm."

"I don't expect you to understand."

Hearing a groan, Jennie's gaze swung from the map to the couch behind them and the figure lying there. Sal. Jennie sucked in a deep breath. His hands and legs had been secured and he lay on his side—unconscious.

Jennie ran to his side and automatically checked for a pulse. "What have you done to him?"

"He's fine, Jennie. I had to give him something to keep him quiet. I'll have to do the same with you."

"Why? You can't possibly think you'll get away with this."

"Oh, I'll get away all right. Tomorrow night—after the funeral. I have a team coming in to help me pack all this up."

"Mary knows I'm here. She'll get worried. My parents are coming."

"Yes, I know." She gave Jennie a wan smile. "I'll tell them you were here and that you left right after tea. The last I saw of you, you were heading back toward the lake. I'll help look for you, of course. It's terrifying to know the killer is still out there—stalking innocent victims. None of us is safe anymore." Tears filled her eyes, creating the picture of empathy.

She looked so sincere, Jennie almost believed her. Licking her dry lips, she said, "Agent Tucker will be here soon—to question you about Sal. He'll figure it out."

"Oh, I don't think so. Agent Tucker is a very attractive man, don't you think? He sees me as everyone else does—a poor, weak, frail little woman. People are very protective of me, you know. He's been especially kind. I'll invite him to look around. There's no way he'll find this place."

"He suspects you."

"Does he?" She raised her eyebrows in surprise. "Then I'll have to be more convincing." Christine stepped over to where Jennie was standing. "I don't have time for any more chitchat. As you can see, I still have a lot of packing to do. Put your hands behind your back."

"No." Jennie stepped to the side. If she could distance herself enough, maybe she could reach the door. Jennie took another step back, then another.

Christine's sinister smile gave Jennie little hope of getting away, but she had to try. Jennie made it as far as the stairs. Christine grabbed her shirt and yanked her back. Jennie spun around and kicked, landing a forceful blow to the older woman's knee. She screeched and charged again. Jennie scrambled up the stairs. Christine grabbed her ankle and sent her sprawling.

"No!" Jennie screamed one loud, piercing scream before Christine pinned her to the floor, face buried in the carpet, muffling any further sound.

"You may as well give it up, Jennie. You're no match for me."

Jennie struggled, but it was no use. She could think of only one way to fight her. Jennie went limp. Closing her eyes, she pretended she'd lost consciousness. Maybe she couldn't fight, but she wasn't about to give up and she wasn't going to make it easy.

"Jennie?" Christine loosened her hold on Jennie and felt for a pulse. Apparently satisfied she hadn't killed her prey, she moved away.

Ear to the floor, Jennie listened for Christine's footfall. Had she gone for something to tie her up with? Or was she waiting for Jennie to make a move?

A car pulled into the driveway. Where was Christine? Jennie peered between half-closed eyelids. Christine had gone to the window. She swore and spun around, then strode back to where Jennie lay. Eyes closed again, Jennie continued to play unconscious. Car doors slammed. Who was it? Judging by the derogatory names Christine had used and the tone of her voice, Jennie thought it might be Agent Tucker or Sheriff Parker—or both. No matter who it was, Jennie knew this was her best chance of getting help.

Christine grabbed Jennie's ankles and dragged her into the hall.

The doorbell rang. Jennie screamed and kicked as hard as she could, connecting with Christine's thighs.

"Shut up, you idiot. You'll ruin everything."

The door burst open. Agent Tucker, gun drawn, yelled for

Christine to stop. "Get away from her—now!" The moment Christine let go, Jennie rolled onto her stomach, and despite the pain in her neck and shoulders, she got to her feet.

"She's Sonja," Jennie panted. "She has guns and bombs in a command center in the basement. Sal's down there." She quickly filled them in on the details.

Christine leaned forward against the wall while Tess patted her down, read her her rights, and handcuffed her.

Christine straightened and held her head high. "It won't end with me, you know. Someone will come in and take my place, just like I took over for the last Sonja. You can arrest me, but you'll never end the movement. Never. We won't stop until every animal is safe and free."

Jennie shuddered at the vehemence in her voice.

"That may be"—Tess holstered her gun—"but at least we've got you. That's a start."

"This is your fault, Jennie McGrady. You'll have the blood of murdered animals all over the world on your hands."

"Enough!" Tess turned to the FBI agent. "Go ahead and check on Sal. I'll stay up here with her."

Jennie led Tucker down to the hidden room. He untied Sal while Jennie called for an ambulance.

"You took a big chance coming here, Jennie," Tucker said when she hung up.

"I know. I came to bring her a casserole. I should have left right away. I underestimated her. I was just going to look at her car and leave. I really don't think she meant to kill us. She was planning to leave tomorrow after the funeral."

Tucker shook his head. "I doubt she intended to take you along. She'd have left you here, but how long do you think you'd have survived in this hole?"

Jennie grimaced. "Yeah, but it wouldn't have been her fault."

"What?"

"It would have been mine for coming here. That's how she justifies what she does. It's never her fault."

He put in a call to another agent asking him to bring an officer in to examine and gather the evidence. "We shouldn't have any trouble putting her away with all of this. And unless I miss my guess, her computer system will give us access to other key members. We may even be able to thwart some of their plans."

"I'm glad to hear that. Scott will be too. Do you think Aleshia knew about her mother? It still seems impossible for her to have kept it a secret so long."

"Amazingly enough, I don't think she had a clue." Agent Tucker cast her a lopsided grin. "Much as I hate to say it, Jennie, without you, we might not have caught Christine. She covered her tracks well and she was right about one thing. Even with a search warrant, we might not have found her little hiding place."

"I'm just glad you showed up," Jennie said. "Which reminds me, why did you come?"

"Wanted to ask her a few questions about Sal's working for them. We thought he might have an affiliation with ARM and been sent to scope out the place. I also thought he was the one who ambushed us."

Jennie tucked a strand of hair behind her ear. "Christine did that. She also instigated the release."

Jennie hung around until Tess had taken her prisoner and the ambulance had come to get Sal. He'd be fine, they'd said. Crystal and her mother would meet them at the hospital. Agent Tucker offered her a ride back to the Bergstroms' and Jennie took it.

———

Four days later, Jennie entered the Trinity pool area and dove into the clear, inviting water. She'd finished school early and wanted to get in some extra lap time. Except for her and Coach Dayton, who was holed up in her office grading papers, the place was deserted.

Jennie swam her laps with far less enthusiasm than she should have had. The investigation still weighed heavy on her mind. Bob Sutherland's killer was behind bars. Sonja had been captured along with a hundred or more commandos who'd terrorized the fur farming industry over the years. Aleshia and Crystal were no longer ARM members.

After her ordeal with Christine, Jennie had gone back to the Bergstroms'. Mary blamed herself for sending Jennie to her near death, which was fine with Jennie as it meant she wouldn't get into trouble with her parents. Instead, they hailed her a hero. She'd even gotten a call from the Fur Commission commending her actions.

As a bonus, Tess Parker had called the day before to tell Jennie she was leaving Thompson. Her husband had called the day after reading about the bust to tell her about a job opening for a police chief in a small town east of Seattle. If everything went well, she'd be back with her family within the month.

Everything had turned out well, except one small detail— Scott Chambers. She hadn't heard from him and still had no idea where he was. Calls to the FBI proved fruitless. Last night she finally resorted to calling Gram, who said she and J.B. would look into the matter.

Finishing her laps, Jennie hit the wall and started to pull herself up. She saw a jean-clad leg, a leather hiking boot, and a flash of white before her head went under again. Jennie struggled for a moment, then reached up, grasping the hand that held her down. Bracing her feet against the pool wall, she pulled her attacker off balance and into the water.

Hearing his yelp, Jennie hoisted herself out of the pool. A wide smile played on her lips as she watched him right himself and grab the edge of the pool.

"Hey, what did you do that for?" Scott shook the water out of his dark hair. "You got my cast wet."

"Serves you right, sneaking up on me like that." She wrapped a towel around herself and stepped back when he reached for her leg.

"Okay, you win." He dragged himself out of the water. "No more games. You don't play fair."

"Me!" Jennie gaped at him. "You're the one who tried to drown me."

Scott straightened and smiled at her.

Jennie smiled back. "I missed you."

"Yeah?"

"So why didn't you call?" She grabbed another towel to dry her hair.

"FBI wanted me to lie low for a few days to be sure I wasn't in any more danger."

"You could have let me know. . . ."

"Jennie." His green eyes met hers, and she forgot all about her anger. She forgot about everything except that he was standing there looking so cute and . . .

His arms went around her and in the next instant he was kissing her.

"You're wet," she said when they finally drew apart.

Scott tipped his head back and laughed. "Thanks to you."

She glanced at his still-dripping cast. "Sorry about that."

"Hey, no problem—it's been through worse. But if you're really broken up about it, you can take me to the clinic after practice and stay with me till I get a new one, then take me out to dinner. I want to hear your side of the story."

"You're on!"